US
AGAINST
THEM

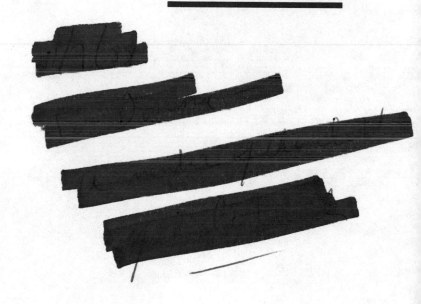

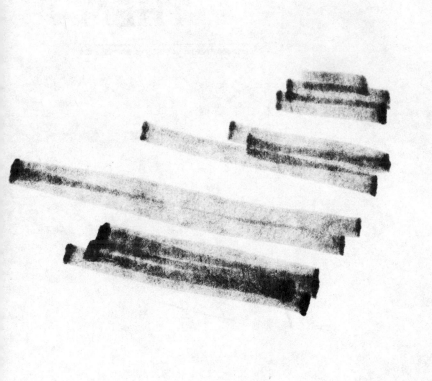

US
AGAINST
THEM

Michael French

BANTAM BOOKS
TORONTO • NEW YORK • LONDON • SYDNEY • AUCKLAND

US AGAINST THEM

A Bantam Book / November 1987

Library of Congress Cataloging-in-Publication Data

French, Michael, 1944–
    Us against them.

    Summary: Sixteen-year-old Reed, the leader of a club with a reputation for bucking adult authority, makes a gesture of defiance by taking his friends camping in the Adirondacks, only to find his band collapsing into dissension and violence.
    [1. Camping—Fiction. 2. Adirondack Mountains (N.Y.)—Fiction. 3. Clubs—Fiction. 4. Friendship—Fiction.]
    I. Title.
PZ7.F88905Us 1987   [Fic]   87-14465
    ISBN 0-553-05440-6

Published simultaneously in the United States and Canada

PRINTED IN THE UNITED STATES OF AMERICA

FG   0 9 8 7 6 5 4 3 2 1

To Sue "Nana" Green,
for her support and love

US
AGAINST
THEM

1

Fireworks again. Devon Beaupre
skidded his ten-speed to a stop on the bluff and let his long
arms dangle over the handlebars. A hundred yards below,
on the crooked finger of a dirt road that led to the
Adirondacks, Reed Higdon and Otis Foley were already
out of Otis's pickup. The sheriff had pulled them over with
a blast of his siren.

The voices were too distant to make out, but even
without his glasses Devon got the picture. That cheap-shot
artist Sheriff Covington had his ticket book out—what was
it this time? Busted taillight? Loose muffler? No license?
Give the sheriff credit, he was a genius at getting under
your skin. Everyone in the club felt frustrated by Sheriff
Covington. Devon wondered if there'd ever be a solution.

Suddenly he remembered the bazooka he'd seen in one of Benjy's soldier-of-fortune magazines. Devon hoisted the invisible weapon to his shoulder. For a moment he stared at Reed through the sight. The tall, well-built body. The intense brown eyes. The strong jaw. Then Devon quickly swung the weapon, drew a bead on the sheriff's car, and squeezed the trigger.

As the three figures circled each other below, Devon pedaled on to the clubhouse that was ten minutes away. He couldn't help his friends, anyway, and the truth was, the sheriff intimidated him. Devon was sure that in Sheriff Covington's former life he was either Attila the Hun or a Marine drill sergeant. Still, Devon wondered if Reed could talk his way out of the ticket. Otis had been driving, but surely Reed would take charge. That was his nature, and Devon thought Reed could accomplish almost anything, even against an enemy like Covington.

The town of Olancha receded behind him in shimmering waves of afternoon heat. Devon felt a brief flicker of hope that one day it would be behind him forever. Olancha—his hometown and a microscopic dot on an upstate New York map—didn't have much to say for itself. It sat at the base of the soaring and rugged Adirondacks like a movie set—a few dozen residential streets, a mobile home park, a local bank, a church, a doctor's office, a small lumber company, a movie theater that was now permanently shut down, a dry goods store, a grocery store, two coffee shops, and the Do-Drop-In Bar and Lounge that was never empty. Devon guessed there were lots of little towns like this across America. But their residents probably didn't have to suffer a two-man sheriff's office that had nothing better to do than keep the locals in line on Saturday nights or set radar traps on the nearby interstate—or pick on teenagers. In Wayne Junction, twenty miles east, the junior high and high school were a refuge for kids nine months of the year. It was the other three months when Devon and his friends went bananas.

That's what he liked to complain about to good old Hugo, anyway. The editor of the Wayne Junction *Herald* had first taken an interest in Devon when, last year, he'd applied for a summer intern job. The *Herald* had no intern program—the paper was too small—but Hugo had liked what Devon had written for the high-school paper and encouraged him to keep in touch, even to send in articles for the *Herald* to consider. A dreamer, Devon had flooded Hugo with stories. A few pieces had actually been printed, which had made Devon and his parents proud. But Devon had been disappointed, too. *His* favorite stories, about Olancha driving kids crazy, were not Hugo's. Two years ago the sheriff had managed to close the Olancha municipal pool, last summer it was the movie theater. Now there was a new bicycle ordinance that kept Devon and his friends off the main street from nine to five during summer months. Town merchants thought bike traffic disturbed visiting campers and hunters, the heart of the summer economy. "Hey, what about us?" Devon had complained to Hugo. "Kids spend money, too, don't they? Isn't it an insult enough we can't find summer jobs around here? Isn't there a story for your paper in all this?"

Hugo, who liked to sit in his small, cluttered office with his hands folded across his plump stomach, was sympathetic. The look on his ruddy face showed that. But he was

3

also practical. "Devon, I know Olancha's slow-moving, and you and your pals get the short end of the sheriff's stick, but that's not quite newsworthy. And the sheriff hasn't bothered you that much, has he? Listen, the summer will be over in a wink . . ."

Devon liked Hugo—the editor was one of the rare adults Devon felt ever really listened—but sometimes he thought Hugo just didn't understand.

As Devon neared the clubhouse he watched the construction crew finishing the new off-ramp from the interstate. Tomorrow it was supposed to be asphalted. Sheriff Covington would probably have a ribbon-cutting ceremony for the official opening. The town merchants thought the new exit was the best thing to happen to Olancha since hunting season. But new business won't change the town's character for the better, Devon thought as he rolled his bike in front of the abandoned gas station that had become their clubhouse.

Other bikes were already parked next to Otis's battered pickup, which had easily beaten Devon. A monument of rusting oilcans and car parts was piled next to the inactive gas pumps. On the exterior the building didn't look much better than the grounds, but that was the beauty of it. Nobody from town could guess what was inside.

When the gas station had been deserted a few years ago it had been Reed's idea to turn it into their private clubhouse. At garage sales in Wayne Junction Otis, Devon, and Reed had bought a noisy old refrigerator, a black-and-white TV, a phonograph, some throw rugs, even a few paintings for the walls. The process had taken almost a year, working weekends, but together they'd made the gas

4

station into something of their own, something no one could take from them. Now seven kids belonged to the club. They might not feel the same about everything, but one thing was certain—they all couldn't stand the small-town mentality of Olancha. They were seven strong, and glad to have each other.

Devon untied the wrapped cake from his bike rack and moved inside with anticipation. The room was decorated with streamers, twisting along ceiling rafters and down walls. Marcy Creighton had made enough fried chicken for the whole town, which happy-go-lucky Otis was already munching on. Reed and Otis had brought beer and soft drinks. Benjy McCloud, the youngest and smallest and lazier than a pregnant cat, had contributed paper plates and napkins. The twins, Amber and Jade Sheedy, stood over a mountain of tossed salad. Marcy burst into mock applause at Devon's cooking ability when he unwrapped his cake.

"Over here," Reed called as he held up two candles for the cake. In cutoffs and a T-shirt that revealed his hefty shoulders and bulging legs, Reed looked like the mountain trekker he often was. For Reed the Adirondacks were a second home. Unlike Reed, Devon was no adventurer; he was lanky and not particularly agile. And he was content to sit over his typewriter or to read a good book.

"I know we're not here to celebrate the opening of a fast-food place," Reed announced to the others, "or the demise of the sheriff's rules"—he made a joking face as he lit the candles—"but what we're here for is more important."

"Three cheers for our second anniversary!" Otis cried.

"One for all, all for one!" Benjy chimed in.

Together the seven blew out the candles.

"I thought you might wear a tux for such an important occasion," Marcy teased Reed as the cake was cut and passed around.

"I'm saving it for when I take you to the senior prom, Ms. Creighton." Reed looked as if he expected a rise from Marcy. But she said nothing, and her lean, pretty, sculpted face didn't reveal her thoughts.

"So what happened with the sheriff?" Devon asked Reed. "Did you worm your way out?"

"What do you think?" Reed answered.

Devon peeked at Otis. No help there.

"Come on . . ." Reed pushed him playfully. "If you had to bet—"

"Okay, assuming I were a betting man, which I'm not," Devon went along, "a buck says you saved Otis's hide."

"You're smart, Devon."

"Yeah, but freedom for a price," Otis interjected.

Reed shrugged cavalierly and told Devon what had happened. To get Otis off the hook, Reed had promised the sheriff his souvenir basketball, the one the Lakers had all signed the year they'd beaten the Boston Celtics in Boston Garden for the championship. Otherwise, the ticket would have cost Otis sixty dollars he didn't have. Covington didn't see the gesture as a bribe, just a way of paying the ticket. Devon knew how much that ball meant to Reed. The lightning-quick guard was Mr. Basketball in upstate New York, and was expected to make all-state as a senior next year. He had high hopes of winning a college scholarship. Still, Devon wasn't surprised Reed had done Otis the favor. He was always making sacrifices to help others.

"Hey," Otis shouted over the party noise, "anybody think the sheriff's department will remember us and send flowers to our party?"

Devon watched as a knowing smile inched up Reed's face. The sheriff considered Reed a royal pain and trouble-maker. Even the parents of some of the kids in the club wondered why an otherwise charming, talented young man like Reed wasted his time making unnecessary waves. But Devon didn't see them as unnecessary. If you were a teenager in Olancha you got as much respect as a goldfish. When the pool and the movie theater had been closed Reed had circulated petitions to get them reopened; when that failed he'd attended town council meetings to protest. The sheriff hated him for bucking authority. Devon had always felt that Covington was waiting for the day to get even with Reed. Some adults in town were sympathetic to the teenagers and even to the club's cause, but not enough to make a move against Covington or the council. People seemed to accept the status quo.

Devon had just slipped one of his rock LPs on the phonograph when something stirred outside. He rose cautiously. No one bothered them here. The knock hardly sounded urgent; no one else had even heard it. Opening the door Devon stared at Covington in his starched beige uniform. The trim, middle-aged sheriff managed a little grin of superiority.

"Done a nice job on your clubhouse," he volunteered as he peeked over Devon's shoulder, taking an interest for the first time. "What's the party for?" The music was suddenly turned off and the others mushroomed behind Devon. Reed sliced his way to the front.

7

"What do you want?" Reed said. The tone was civil but with an edge of defiance. "This is a private party. Unless we're breaking some law . . ."

"No," came the thoughtful reply, "not yet." A thin brown envelope rose up from nowhere, and passed into Reed's hand like a baton in a relay.

"That's for all of you. And nothing personal." Covington strolled to his car, which, as usual, was immaculate. "Sure am sorry to be the bearer of bad news," he offered, twisting his head back.

"What news?" Reed demanded as he tore open the envelope.

"Sometimes local governments have to do things for the good of their town," Covington said. "For instance, they have the right to condemn property, even if it's private. Ever heard of the right of eminent domain?"

"What about it?" Devon spoke up uneasily. He knew the term. His eyes were fixed on Covington as the car motor whined.

"Got a new exit coming off the interstate. Lots of additional traffic for Olancha. Town council decided we need a wider and better road into town. . . ."

Incredulous, Devon looked at Reed, who finally gazed up from the letter. His face had paled.

"What I'm trying to tell you," Covington spelled out for the stubborn faces, "is that some properties will be in the way of the new road. Your clubhouse is going to be torn down."

2

"**H**ow can he?" Benjy demanded as everyone watched the sheriff's tires spit up a defiant plume of dust. The thirteen-year-old looked to Reed for a denial.

"He can do it," Reed answered. He half-sat on the table and read the letter out loud. Anger swept over him as he explained the document. The town of Olancha was condemning the gas station. By July first it would be razed, and road construction would begin. The club had two weeks to remove its possessions and vacate the premises. The decision of the town council could not be appealed; there were no alternative road sites from the off-ramp.

Devon squeezed his hands angrily in his pockets and

roamed around the room. "When we found this gas station they promised no one could take it away from us. They lied to us. We've been betrayed."

"We've never asked this town for very much, never more than what we've been entitled to," Otis said. "Now we don't even have a place to meet. This stinks."

"Let's see an attorney," Marcy suggested to Reed.

"Fine, but there's none in Olancha."

"Then Wayne Junction."

"How are we going to afford one?" Jade asked. "And I'll bet there's nothing a lawyer can do." Her face had gone white, making her freckles stand out. She usually didn't talk as much as her twin, but she felt she had to speak up. "Maybe we should meet with the town council."

"Dream on," Devon said. "Just like we protested everything else?" He combed his fingers through his hair. "I'm going to Hugo again. Maybe he'll finally concede there's a story. We could get lots of public sympathy over this. We could force the town to change its mind."

"Why don't we just build another clubhouse?" Amber asked.

"Where? With what?" Devon said. "And just to have it taken away from us again?"

Reed raised himself from the table. His anger was slow to dissolve. "Devon's right—the club has been betrayed," he said in a tight voice. "But going to the *Herald* for help is just more dreaming. Hugo's never done anything about our reasonable complaints. Why should this be different? The fact is, the town isn't going to provide for us. That means we have to take care of ourselves."

"What do we do?" Benjy asked. In his camouflage fatigues he looked ready for battle.

"I know of another clubhouse," Reed said quietly.

Otis looked skeptical. "Must be in a pretty secret place. Mars or Pluto?"

Reed gave a wry smile. "Actually, not far from our backyard. In the Adirondacks. It's an old cabin. Some mountain man abandoned it. I was there once. It's perfect—isolated, near this stream swollen with trout, facing a gorgeous meadow . . . ."

Marcy shook her head. "We can't just ride our bikes up—"

"That's the whole point," Reed said. "It's far enough away so no one can bother us. A good day's hike. State forest land. Covington has no jurisdiction anyway."

Benjy frowned. "What do you mean? We're going to hike up there and then hike back?"

"Let's spend a few days together. Just club members. By ourselves. Un-dis-turbed," Reed pronounced each syllable distinctly. "It's summer, isn't it? Except for Otis, has somebody got a job?"

"Screw my job at the garage," Otis declared in his nonchalant way. "My brother can take care of things for a few days. When do we take off?"

"We'll clear this place out this afternoon, then leave first thing in the morning." Reed was feeling more pleased with his idea by the minute.

"I guess my folks would let me go," Marcy allowed.

"Not ours."

Eyes jumped to Amber. "Why not?" Reed asked. "We've taken day trips in the Adirondacks."

"But now we're talking about a few days. Our dad doesn't exactly trust you or like you, Reed. Ever since you had the club and other kids boycott his store because he was against reopening the movie theater—"

"We did what we had to do. Just like we're doing now." Reed flashed Amber a look. He didn't like it that she would take her dad's side against the club's—what about loyalty to her friends? What about just having a good time together? At home, by Amber's and Jade's own admissions, Mr. Sheedy was a tyrant, just like his buddy, the sheriff.

"If it weren't for our mom siding with us," Amber argued, "Jade and I wouldn't be allowed in the club at all. Asking for permission to go on an overnight all together is pushing it. You all know our dad's temper. . . ."

"You have to stick up for yourselves," Reed said, impatient that no one was seeing the real issue. "And we all have to stick together. Come on, no one takes us seriously. We're treated like we have no rights, no feelings, like no one wants or needs us. It's time to show these adults that we don't need *them*." Reed listened to the cadence of his voice, the mingling of logic and emotion. He meant every word.

"My folks won't object," Devon said eagerly. He thought again of going to Hugo, but Reed was probably right about it being more wheel spinning. Hugo wouldn't print the story. Reed's adventure would at least mean doing something.

"Mine will go along, too," Benjy threw in.

Reed felt better, vindicated, as he gazed at the twins.

The two girls looked at each other uncertainly. "All right," Amber promised, feeling the pressure, "we'll ask at least."

"The trip'll be a ball," Reed tried to give them courage. The others did, too. Reed was confident everything would work out. For all the twins' misgivings, Mr. Sheedy would probably be relieved not to have his daughters or the rest of the club around for a few days. Reed delivered a loud belch to break the tension. Amid the laughter he took a pencil from behind his ear and began a list of camping supplies.

The air was still and warm. On his front porch Reed lingered to study the twinkling lights of Olancha. It was almost midnight, but he didn't want to go into his house yet. Tomorrow he would be looking back at the place where he was sitting now, but no one would be able to spot him. The thought pleased him. He loved the solitude of the mountains and went climbing often by himself. He just had to escape. The town was full of hypocrites, and the indifference he felt from adults disgusted him.

When Reed had told his father about leaving for a trip the next day, Sam Higdon hadn't understood the need to claim a new clubhouse. "The idea of a club is a little juvenile for a sixteen-year-old, isn't it?" his father had asked. "All this talk about loyalty and togetherness sounds a little too rah-rah."

Reed had just turned away. He'd given up arguing with his father years ago, in Pittsburgh, not long after his mother had been killed in an auto accident. His father had

13

never particularly been someone to look up to, and in trying to raise Reed alone, he'd floundered. He could never comfort Reed for the death, never knew what to say to his son. Reed had wanted to feel closer, yet his father was always busy with one inconsequential thing or another. Over the years he'd brought home a stream of women friends for the companionship he wouldn't accept from his son. None of the women took much interest in Reed. Sometimes he'd felt like he didn't even belong in his house. After a while, angry, he'd tried to forget he had a dad.

Reed gave a final glance to the inky blackness that was the mountains, and drifted into the simple two-bedroom rental. His father was sprawled on the sofa, eyes closed to a flickering television, lost in dreamland. That's where he usually was. His father liked to ramble about his great life in the sixties when John F. Kennedy was president and everyone felt they were going to change the world for the better. So much talk. Reed's father was basically a hippie who'd never changed anything except his job and address. After his mother's death, Reed had been bounced from town to town until finally in Olancha there'd been forestry work for his dad.

All the moving had been hard. Just when Reed got to know and like a teacher, the relationship ended. It was even tougher with kids. Knowing that a friendship wouldn't last, through no fault of his, made Reed feel helpless. At least now he had the club and the strong ties he'd never found at home. To be a leader, to be in charge of others, made him feel good about himself.

A part of Reed always feared his father would move again. For survival he had learned to rely on himself because he knew he couldn't trust his fate to anyone. Maybe he wasn't a class brain like Devon, but he was sharp in his own way and he had the ability to make himself popular. Devon and Otis had suggested he run for student-body president in the fall. He hoped kids liked him not just for his personality but for his principles, the ones that the club stood for, the principles that his father only paid lip service to: loyalty, resisting hypocrisy, working hard to accomplish your goals. It was important to Reed not to compromise. That's why he knew he was going to make something of himself, the "something" his father only talked about.

In his bedroom he picked up his Lakers' basketball, the one he now owed the sheriff, and spun it on the tip of his finger like a top. He counted up to *fifteen Mississippi* and the ball was still in orbit. A Harlem Globetrotter couldn't do it any better. Reed smiled. He loved basketball. He was good at baseball and track, too, but basketball was special. He liked its requirements—quickness, finesse, thinking on one's feet, the element of surprise. He rolled the basketball into a corner of the living room. The sheriff could pick up the ball from his father anytime. Reed was no welsher, and anyway, one day he'd find a way to win it back.

Methodically, he began to haul his cache of camping gear piecemeal from his closet to the front porch: sleeping bag and pad, ground cloth, plenty of rope, cookware, first-aid kit, pocketknife, insect repellent, ax, collapsible shovel, hammer, canteen, waterproof matches, fishing line—

15

and extra clothes, wool, not cotton, because if it rained or got cold wool would hold its warmth. He made a final check. Whatever he couldn't fit into his backpack he dropped into a poncho and wrapped into a bundle, then tied it to the backpack frame. For an early start the next day, gear and food had to be brought over to the clubhouse that night.

Reed had slipped into the straps of his backpack and was halfway across his yard when he remembered. Just in case, he thought, returning to the house. He had a hunting license, and though only small game were in season, that was all he'd be after. In his father's room the gun cabinet was padlocked, but Reed knew the combination. The lock lifted quietly from its hasp and the glass door creaked open. His fingers squeezed around a black Colt .45 revolver that he'd shot often in practice, though his father didn't know. He dropped the gun and a dozen rounds into the backpack, hoping they wouldn't be missed.

Reed cut through a vacant lot, skirted past dilapidated stucco and frame houses, and stole silently over the town's back roads. Clouds scudded along to allow glimpses of stars. Around a corner he spotted the twins' two-story house. It was prettier and in better repair than most. Real prosperity for Olancha: large sod yard, fenced-in dog run, plenty of flowers. The Sheedys were owners, not renters.

A light burned from a living room window. Reed could see three figures sitting motionless in the room. What was going on so late? He edged closer, ducking behind the few trees large enough to conceal him. It seemed forever before he reached a window. He peeked above the sill.

16

Amber and Jade sat across from their father. Mr. Sheedy sat silently, his sinewy arms folded over his chest, the muscles in his neck popping out like rope, the pockmarked face set in stone. Reed could feel the girls' uneasiness as the silence continued. His eyes jumped back to their father. A hunter and trekker like Reed, Mr. Sheedy was quiet, aloof, and didn't like anyone interfering with his family. He wasn't totally antisocial, Reed knew, and certainly wasn't selfish. He worked with several state charities and donated a little money, too. Mr. Sheedy's best friend was the sheriff. Reed knew they shared the same opinion of him and the club—they hated kids who bucked adult authority. Reed would never admit it to his friends, but Mr. Sheedy scared him. Covington was more cool and detached—Sheedy was emotional. Reed was careful to avoid a confrontation with him. The man's brooding resentment of the boy who influenced his daughters always seemed close to spilling over.

A voice broke the silence. Reed shifted his weight and strained to hear. Amber was explaining the club's plan. Mr. Sheedy's face said he didn't like the idea. Reed suddenly felt guilty—the twins were in the club, his club, and it was his idea which was making their father angry. It was his duty to help them, to explain why they were doing this. But he was chicken. He hated that cowardly feeling. He couldn't stand situations where he wasn't in control. Go on, he told himself, knock on the window, do what's right.

The twins' German shepherd began to bark. Eyes in the living room turned to the window. Reed ducked. His heart raced as the window squeaked open. He could feel Mr.

Sheedy's scrutinizing gaze sweeping over the yard. The few seconds felt like hours, then the window shuddered down. Reed caught his breath, crept along the side of the house, and scrambled away.

Mr. Sheedy wouldn't have listened to me, anyway, he told himself. He tried to forget his feelings of cowardice and hurried on to his destination. Other chances to help the twins would come up. He was sure of it.

3

The sun dipped behind the jagged peaks to the west just as the cabin rose into view. Bathed in sweat, Devon gave a whoop of glee and dropped in the cool grass. The abandoned cabin was right where Reed had promised—dead-center north by northwest from Olancha, nine hours of well-paced hiking. A late-afternoon breeze stirred the surrounding spruces as the others clambered up the last hill. Birds wheeled noiselessly in the air. They'd all made it, and in good spirits, even the twins. Devon had worried that Amber and Jade wouldn't be coming, but they were there. They said that after begging and pleading with their father, somehow they'd gotten their way.

Slipping out of his backpack, Devon angled his neck up.

Long ridges of blue-green foliage alternated with austere peaks of gray rock. One or two peaks still had crowns of snow, pinkish in the fading light. The cabin faced a U-shaped meadow that was flanked by granite outcroppings and towering forests of hardwoods, hemlock, and white pines. Devon wished he'd brought his camera. Purple and pink wildflowers carpeted the endless meadow, uninterrupted by campers' tents or other cabins. They really were all alone. No one could tell them what to do.

Devon cleaned his glasses on his shirttail. The only thing he missed having was his typewriter. He wanted to describe the great feeling of freedom he felt. But maybe it was good to take a holiday. He was always writing. It was a way of escaping the monotony of the town. But it was more than that. He wanted his ideas to be read. At school some kids thought he took himself too seriously with his investigative reporting and getting published in the *Herald,* accusing him of trying to make a name for himself. Devon shook his head at that one. What was wrong with a little ambition? He didn't want to be an unknown nobody buried forever in Olancha, did he? Reed understood his dreams perfectly. Devon liked to share his ideas, his writing, with his friend. Reed was even more ambitious than Devon, and they both knew that having ambition wasn't bad. Devon realized again how lucky he was to have Reed for a friend.

"No rest for the weary," Reed kidded as his shadow darted over Devon in the grass. An avalanche of gear spilled out of Reed's opened poncho. Under his direction everyone was assigned a chore. Devon placed rocks in a circle for a fire and sorted out pots and pans. He hoped he

looked like he knew what he was doing. Even though he'd
been born in the lap of the Adirondacks, he knew as much
about camping and wilderness skills as he did about flying
a 747. The danger and uncertainty of the mountains had
always intimidated him. He blamed his parents. Whenever
they finished up in their coffee shop, their idea of escape
was curling up with a crossword puzzle or finding another
couple to play bridge. Devon had been raised on their
stories of men swallowed alive in blizzards, blown off
peaks by treacherous winds, just plain getting lost. He
never understood why they'd settled in Olancha in the first
place. They'd never taken advantage of the gorgeous sur-
roundings they lived in. Devon's biggest adventures before
he'd started going on hikes with the club had been a
couple of fishing outings. It was almost embarrassing to be
so awkward and uncomfortable in the outdoors. Maybe I'll
never be as skilled as Reed, he thought suddenly, but I'm
taller and stronger than my father now, and it's time to
learn new things.

Devon coaxed a fire out of kindling but didn't tell the
others it took him a dozen matches. As the twins boiled
spaghetti, he peeked into the cabin. Marcy had already laid
out the sleeping bags on the dirt floor. The door had been
ripped off, leaving rusty hinges, and the windows had no
glass left. The stone fireplace looked like it might be made
to work. How long had the cabin been abandoned? Devon
didn't know much about mountain men. Town folktales
included recluses or squatters on state land. Occasionally
Devon would see a mountain man in Olancha buying
supplies, and last year the sheriff had arrested one poor
loner for burglarizing the laundromat. It had made Coving-

ton an instant hero. Devon didn't think of the mountain men as threatening but they weren't friendly either.

"Here, here," Otis announced when dinner was finally ready. Everybody sat around the fire and raised their drinking cups. The sky was beginning to cloud over but enough daylight remained to study Otis's wry grin. Devon envied Otis for his looseness. Nothing fazed him. Otis's parents had died in a light aircraft accident, which left Otis in the care of his relaxed, older brother.

"A toast to the club!" Otis declared. "And our new clubhouse!"

"And to no one hassling us—ever again," Reed declared.

"To peace and harmony," seconded Jade.

Marcy jumped to her feet. "To seven stalwart adventurers!"

Reed began to sing a variation on the school fight song, off-key, substituting *Gang of Seven* for *Matadors*. Otis emptied his backpack, stuffed with candy and assorted creature comforts, to get to the six-pack. He handed Devon a can. Devon took a few sips, joining in the singing and laughter. After a while he scooted away with his binoculars. From a nearby ridge the distant blur that was Olancha came into focus, enough to see a few lights.

It seemed impossibly far away, another world. He couldn't have been happier. When they'd left town this morning Devon had moved especially fast. Every few hundred yards he had glanced back, certain that his parents would be at his heels, changing their minds and wanting him home for chores or to help in the restaurant. Reed was right, it was great to get away. Devon thought he disliked Olancha more than the others did—he had higher stan-

22

dards, and he was more judgmental—but he didn't broadcast most of his complaints. He expressed them mainly to his friends and in his personal writing. He didn't have the confidence to make waves the way Reed did. Why focus just on Olancha? he rationalized. It wasn't the only screwed-up town on the planet.

Last spring, when he'd been a finalist in a national science fair, he'd flown to Los Angeles with high hopes. But competitive teachers who judged the entries had favored their own students. His cousin in Connecticut bragged to Devon about how he cheated on tests. In Chicago his uncle had just been indicted for tax evasion. Devon knew he was smart enough to see the injustices of life but not smart—or bold—enough to change them. He wasn't like Reed. But one day he hoped he would be. He thought of the club. They were all friends. They respected each other and shared the same values. If the rest of civilization were destroyed tomorrow, the seven would carry on just fine up here. Sure, his parents were important, but the club seemed like his family, too.

Devon shook off his pensive mood and turned in early with the others. Through a chink in the roof he could see a sliver of moon. He wrestled uncomfortably against the cool nylon sleeping bag, wishing he'd brought a pad for it. The others were already asleep, lumpy outlines scattered across the floor, arms flung in twisted positions. The hike had exhausted his body but his mind wouldn't turn off. He squirmed out of his sleeping bag and fumbled into his clothes. A short walk would clear his head.

His flashlight beam wobbled ahead over the gently sloping valley, highlighting the flowers that were cool and moist under his bare feet. The air smelled of pine. He felt something even more imposing and formidable about the mountains than he did in the day, making him conscious of his solitude. The world seemed to grow bigger when the light left it. For a moment he let himself be swallowed in the darkness as he perched on a fallen log. Darkness and peace.

Something clicked behind him.

Devon jerked his flashlight around, but his thumb couldn't find the switch. When it did, there was nothing to see. Reed had mentioned that elk, timber wolves, and moose no longer roamed the mountains. But deer and beaver were abundant, and small game held their own. He was more curious than afraid.

The noise came again. Farther away this time. His eyes strained in the darkness, beyond the point where his flashlight beam weakened and dissolved. Then he noticed—as if it had always been there—a small pinprick of light, moving rapidly, out of the valley toward the forests. Another flashlight surely. Reed or Otis? Unlikely. He'd left everyone asleep in the cabin.

Devon slid off the log and followed. Was he asking for trouble? The pinprick of light suddenly died. It had to be a person. He stared into the void, perplexed and disappointed. Pivoting, he aimed his flashlight in the direction from which he'd come. The trees didn't look familiar, or rather they all did. Shadows, limbs, twisted trunks. He might as well have been wearing a blindfold. A wind rustled the trees, singing as it gusted over the ridges around him. Damn, how was he going to get back? Should he yell for Reed and the others? That would be embarrassing. He groped ahead, hoping his instincts were right.

Footsteps came from behind.

"Who's there?" he called, twisting around with the flashlight. His stomach tightened.

The blackness took on a shape. The man was tall and rangy and broad-shouldered. Devon jerked up his flashlight as if it were a weapon. The beam traveled up his worn jeans and rested on his face. His hair was long and tied in a braid. Devon knew he should be afraid, but he managed to hold the light steady. His gaze drifted to the metal trap flung over the man's shoulder, the sharp teeth silvered by the flashlight. Neither spoke as they studied one another. Devon expected his own composure to shatter, but it was the mountain man who turned first and vanished. Devon couldn't quite forget his face. Aloof, wise, distrustful.

It took almost an hour, and several wrong turns, but Devon found the cabin again.

"You should have stayed clear of him," Reed admonished. "Correction, you should never have been out in the middle of the night."

The morning light was a thin, brittle silver. As the others rustled awake in the cabin, Reed was already fixing coffee and powdered eggs.

"Why?" Devon asked. "The guy wasn't going to hurt me. He was out hunting."

Reed didn't know how to convince Devon. Maybe he was bright, but he was also naive. The mountains were beautiful and a place to have fun, only they weren't a theme park. "Don't you remember that mountain man Covington arrested in town? These guys are strange. You can't trust them. They don't want anything to do with people. That's why they're up here. They're antisocial."

"I know the guy turned his back on society," Devon said, "that's obvious. But so have we in a way. Isn't that a bond?"

"In a way," Reed admitted, "but he's still not one of us. And he doesn't know why we're here."

"What do you mean?"

"We're outsiders. To him, we're no different than anybody else from town. We're out to give him a hard time."

Devon recalled the distrustful face. "Maybe," he conceded.

"Look, Devon, the guy is just different from us. I mean, you wouldn't have him in the club, would you?" Reed joked to end the discussion. He watched Devon glance away. Maybe he'd come down a little hard on his friend, but Reed liked to have the final word. He always did. He couldn't always convince those adults in authority to do what he wanted them to do, but with his friends he got his way. It was important to him. Maybe it was because his father was so laid-back and unconcerned about everything. Maybe he felt he had to prove his abilities to others because, since his mother died, no one seemed to care.

Funny thing about the mountain man, Reed considered as he lounged in the grass. He thinks *we're* the same as everybody in town, while I think *he's* the same: just one more hostile or indifferent face to put up with. Most adults in Olancha lived to watch TV or go drinking, said one thing and did something else—worst of all they treated Reed and the club like *they* were immature. With a grin Reed recalled the slogan his father often repeated as a fond memory of the sixties: "Never trust anyone over thirty."

Reed didn't think of it as a memory. And he lowered the age by ten years.

"What's on the agenda?" Otis asked as the others joined Reed and Devon. He hopped comically on one foot, trying to slip the other into his hiking boot.

"How about a swim after breakfast?" Reed asked. "There's a good-sized pond less than a mile from here." The air was still crisp, but that wouldn't last. Within half an hour it would lose its bite, and the sun would warm the meadow.

Benjy rubbed the sleep out of his eyes. "Isn't the water cold?"

"Nope. Fed by a hot spring. You'll think you've died and gone to heaven."

When they'd cleaned up after breakfast, Reed led them through the meadow. Midway, he stripped off his T-shirt and hung it from his belt loop. The sun hammered down on his broad, tanned shoulders. For a moment he felt swallowed by the immensity of the valley, the unendingness of the mountains, but he would bet anyone he could find his way from one point to the other in the Adirondacks, even without a compass. He was as much at home here as any mountain man.

"How much farther?" a voice suddenly called.

"About ten hours," Reed teased Marcy. He studied her as she stopped to pick a wildflower for her hair. She looked prettier up here than in school, or maybe he was just noticing her more. When they'd first met, Reed had taken no special interest in Marcy, yet they'd ended up being together a lot. Their desks were behind one another in homeroom, they rode the school bus twice a day. Reed

28

had never seriously thought of dating Marcy. She got plenty of attention from boys at school. Their friendship was satisfying enough not to mix in romance. They traded jokes, helped one another with homework, discussed their futures. Marcy had a strong relationship with her parents, her mother especially. In a way, Reed was envious. Maybe it was because of her warm home life that Marcy didn't have concrete plans for leaving town after high school, despite her complaints about Covington and Olancha. Reed teased her about staying on, marrying some local boy from Wayne Junction, never really taking chances with her life. Everyone knew that wasn't for Reed.

Sometimes he thought that Marcy was disappointed that their relationship hadn't progressed, but maybe she didn't see the differences that Reed saw. Besides, he really wasn't involved with any girl. Girls were fun but he couldn't see making a commitment. He didn't feel ready, and he didn't really want to trust anyone with his deepest feelings.

"Last one in—" Benjy shouted. One by one they scaled a final bluff and dropped toward the perfect blue oval of water that sparkled in the sun. Reed stripped to his underwear and plunged in. His head popped up through the water as he beckoned to the others. Marcy hesitated, but after a moment she forgot her modesty and shed her cutoffs and T-shirt. The others followed.

"Take that," Marcy said, shoveling a handful of water at Reed.

"Hey," he warned, "don't sink me." She came at him again, palms extended for all-out war. He grabbed one arm playfully and pulled her to him. Their lips met spontaneously. Surprised, Reed broke away, and wondered if the others had noticed. What did he think he was doing?

The swimming party lasted for an hour. When they'd dried themselves in the sun, lying flat like lizards on the boulders, Reed led them to another pond. Devon had brought along the fishing lines, but the trout were so plentiful you could almost scoop them up with your hands. They traded lines back and forth until everyone had caught something. Devon engineered a makeshift grill while Reed deboned the trout.

"Bon appétit!" Otis clowned as they ate, throwing up a chunk of fish and catching it in his mouth like a seal.

"Let's hear it for table manners!" Devon cheered.

"Hey, Otis, remember when we put that dead fish in Brewster's locker?" Reed would never forget how it had stunk up the hallway. Junior Class President Brewster, an overzealous do-gooder known to rat on fellow students to the faculty, wanted everyone to stay after school to clean the grounds. The fish had only been fair play, Reed had thought.

"That only gets a nine," Benjy said. "The best stunt was when Brewster came in the cafeteria and someone served him warm dog food instead of the stew. Damn if he didn't eat half of it. . . ."

Otis cracked up.

"Gross," Marcy said.

"I was the one who served him," Amber admitted.

"No—" Otis said, as the belly laughs rippled through the group.

"I was afraid to tell anybody. I didn't want to get into trouble."

"You were afraid to tell even us, your good friends?" Reed said.

"Sorry."

"You know what bugged me about that whole incident?" Reed went on. "The vice-principal was determined to find out who did it. Like somebody had committed the crime of the century. Okay, it wasn't so nice, but it was only a joke. The man was obsessed with saving kids from themselves. Let's hear it for the overworked adult mind."

It was dusk when they reached the cabin. The distant outcroppings were purplish and iridescent. Everything's so pretty, so perfect up here, thought Reed. He grabbed a stray pine branch, fastened his blue T-shirt to the end, and jammed the flagpole in a crevice above the cabin door. Then he took a felt marker from his backpack and in bold strokes wrote on the log under the flag:

NO ADULTS ALLOWED

"All-riiiiight!" Otis shouted from where he lounged in the grass.

"Down with Olancha!" added Benjy.

"Hey," Devon declared, "let's make our own town up here. We'll incorporate. Reed for sheriff!"

Thunderous applause and cheering greeted the remark. Reed took a bow, then said, "As elected sheriff, I suggest—not command, you understand—that we start fixing dinner. I'm starved." They scattered to their assigned tasks.

Marcy led Reed into a forest clearing.

"I want to say thank you," she said.

"Yeah, what did I do?"

"Brought us up here. I had my doubts that it would be any different than being in town, or make us feel better. But everything's been great. Everyone feels closer."

31

Marcy dropped her chin on his shoulder. She waited for a response, but Reed offered only an enigmatic smile. She pulled back. At the pond, while she was kissing him, she'd thought she had finally broken through a barrier; now she wasn't sure. For several years Reed had treated her as just a friend, and she hadn't found the way to tell him she wanted something more. She refused to push herself on a boy—she refused to act desperate, because she wasn't—but she'd had a crush on Reed almost since he'd moved to Olancha. She'd never forget that afternoon at the school yard, the first time she saw him, his shirt off as he shot baskets all alone on the blacktop, his body arcing and twisting gracefully in the air, lathered in sweat. She had stood with her fingers plugged into the holes of the chain-link fence, gazing down, feeling a rush of excitement, and though she didn't want to be caught spying, somehow she hoped she would be. But Reed had never even glanced up.

Marcy knew she got easily caught up in boys, but with Reed, despite his indifference, or self-sufficiency, her reaction was a tidal wave. She began fantasizing about him, dreaming about him, pretending they were alone together. At the same time, she resented her helplessness, the blind adoration she felt for him. It didn't seem quite fair unless Reed felt the same way about her. So in the end she'd settled into a pattern of friendship. Eventually she discovered that Reed never went after any girl. He hung back, waiting for girls to pursue him—and when they did, inevitably, he acted like it didn't matter. Mr. Cool. Mr. Mystery. Marcy felt she was as close to Reed as anybody was, even Devon, yet she wondered if she really knew him.

"I think we should get back to the others," Reed finally spoke up.

"What for?" Marcy pulled a handful of blackberries from her pocket and dropped one in Reed's mouth. "What's the matter?" she asked. "You're looking serious all of a sudden."

"Nothing."

"Come on—" She put her arm through his.

"It's just I've had an idea."

Marcy felt a spark of hope. "Don't keep it a secret."

"We're supposed to head home by the day after tomorrow, right? Do you really want to head back? I'm only talking about staying a few more days. What's so urgent at home?"

Marcy wondered if her disappointment showed on her face. She wanted romance, and all Reed was offering was more time in the mountains. She didn't like the suggestion, anyway. It was impossible. "I promised Mom I'd be back on a certain day."

"Explain when we get home. Your mother's a reasonable person—why shouldn't she understand?"

"Maybe she would, but I don't like disappointing her."

"Haven't you ever disappointed her before?" Reed persisted.

"Not on purpose."

"What if there was something else you thought was more important?"

"Like?"

"Staying up here together with your friends. Showing every adult we're independent."

She had wanted him to say, *Staying up here with me.* "I am independent," she answered.

"Really? Are you going to spend the rest of your life in Olancha, like your parents want you to?"

"Look, I haven't made plans one way or the other," she said, a little coolly. She wondered why he was picking on her. She didn't like it. "Maybe I'm not in a big hurry like you seem to be. I think life's a little easier when you don't always buck the system."

Reed glanced away as the silence settled over them uncomfortably. The adoration Marcy usually felt for him, the adoration that made him feel good, was suddenly gone. He didn't get it. Marcy acted like he was attacking her, but he just wanted her to see the issue. As close as she was to her mom, there'd be no damage if she spent a few more days in the mountains. He looked at Marcy again. Did she really think he was a rebel? Maybe by Olancha standards, yet Reed knew he hadn't accomplished much of anything in his life, not yet. Maybe that was his problem. He was frustrated. He remembered kissing Marcy at the pond just hours earlier, how it had surprised him as much as her, how he'd enjoyed it. He was probably frustrated in a lot of ways. Maybe he had to let himself go a little. As their eyes met, Reed let himself experience the feelings he had for Marcy that were deeper than just friendship.

"Is it okay," Reed said when they walked back to the cabin, "if I ask the others what they want to do? We are a club—"

"No, that's fine." Marcy wondered if she wasn't making too much out of Reed's plan. It wasn't like he was asking her never to return home. She pushed away thoughts of her parents as he circled his arm around her. The warmth of his body quickened her breathing.

"I don't know," Benjy allowed after Reed had made

his speech. The flames lit up Benjy's puffy cheeks as he tossed a stick in the fire. Knots of pitch exploded, and the orange flames danced higher. "I know what it comes down to for me. My dad wants me back. I might get the crap beat out of me for being late. . . ."

"But we're making a stand," Reed argued. "Everything we've tried in town has gotten shot down. Up here we can make our own rules, do what we want, have no one to boss us . . ."

"Making a stand?" Amber said. "You make it sound like an act of desperation."

"No, it doesn't." Devon sided with Reed. "It just means we're tired of being pushed around."

Otis nodded wearily. "Hey, it's late. Let's vote."

No one had to be reminded of club rules. The vote had to be unanimous. If it wasn't, Reed knew, they'd stick to the original plan and return when scheduled.

"Otis?" Reed called, crossing his legs. The fire crackled, and in the blackness the wind soughed through the pines.

"Count me in."

"Devon?"

"Definitely yes."

"Benjy?"

"Okay, so I get punished . . ."

Reed felt better. He had momentum now. "Marcy?"

Marcy squirmed as the glances turned toward her. She wasn't so great at handling pressure. She knew that was the way life was sometimes—you had to make decisions, take the consequences—but still she wasn't good at it. She wasn't used to it. There'd never been too much pressure in her life. She lifted her gaze to Reed, and everything she felt for him rushed through her. She'd always had a crush on him. Maybe only by staying in the mountains did she have a chance to turn it into something more. "Count me in," she said.

Reed gave her a reassuring smile. Everything will be all right, he wanted to tell her. Your mother isn't going to call out the National Guard.

"Amberjade?" he called.

The girls' expressions mirrored an identical indecision. The look was just short of fear. Going back to Mr. Sheedy would be no picnic, everyone knew that. Reed felt for the twins—they all did—but wasn't the club important and worth sticking up for?

Finally Amber nodded for both of them.

"Okay, terrific!" Reed exulted. "Hey, nobody worry. Everything's going to be fine."

"Who's worrying?" Otis said. "We're going to make this place into a luxury resort!"

"Here, here!" Devon seconded.

Marcy allowed herself a guarded smile. Reed felt the thrill of power. Everyone had come through. It was beautiful. If not for basketball and college, he suddenly thought, I might never go back to Olancha at all.

5

Devon cleared the last of the weeds around the cabin and reached for his canteen. Benjy and Reed were still working on the fireplace inside; Otis and Marcy were off fishing for dinner. The twins were due back with water. It had been Devon's idea that work be specialized and assigned to teams. Organization and cooperation meant efficiency. Angling his neck to the cloudless sky, Devon realized he couldn't remember the day of the week. Had they been in the mountains six days? Seven? He didn't really care. What was the point of keeping time, anyway? Time was something you worried about when you had deadlines and appointments. He looked at what they'd accomplished. Working together the seven had already replaced the door and window shutters on the cabin and repaired the roof. But it wasn't like they were slaves. Work lasted half a day, then everybody did as they pleased.

The hiking trip and the cabin restoration were similar to another great project the club had joined forces for last summer. Reed had wanted everybody to chip in to buy a junked-out '57 Chevy that Otis had spotted in the Wayne Junction scrap yard. The others said okay, but Marcy hadn't particularly been thrilled. Reed kept kidding her about not being a liberated female until she finally agreed to work on the car. Devon sensed then that Marcy seemed to like Reed as more than a friend, but he'd hoped nothing would develop. The club was better off if everyone just stayed friends. He was sure romance would change things for the worse.

To raise his share for the car, Devon used the money he'd made from selling his articles to Hugo at the *Herald*, and he also sold a leather jacket he loved. The others sacrificed, too. But buying the Chevy had been worth it. Reed had been right as usual. Working together had been terrific. They'd transformed the car into a showpiece that they later resold for a fat profit. What was so typical of Reed was he'd insisted the profits be divided in equal shares. Devon had bought himself a new typewriter and a stereo. The others had splurged too. It was another success for the club.

On impulse Devon picked up his binoculars and clambered up the lichen-covered boulders about the cabin. The sky was as clear as a window pane. Nobody in sight. He would bet the moon some parents or state forest rangers were searching for them, but apparently no one knew about the cabin. That was fine with Devon. His sense of freedom, being on his own, was too intoxicating for him to worry about what he owed his parents. The new, almost reckless feeling gave him a sense of power he'd never experienced before.

He returned the binoculars to his backpack, and looked down at the cabin. Reed had come outside to chop wood. Busy with the ax, he scarcely noticed that Devon had drifted away. He should have told Reed his destination—that was a rule in the mountains, always let someone know where you were going—but Devon wanted to prove something to himself, to Reed as well.

Like the others, Devon looked up to Reed. In small ways he even competed with him—shooting baskets together, fixing up the clubhouse, vying for friends at school. Reed never saw it as competition because there was no serious comparison in skills, personality, or looks. In every department but raw intellect, Reed had him beat hands down. Devon tried to shrug off his feelings of inadequacy, but he wasn't always successful. Sometimes he wondered why Reed even palled around with him. He didn't want to believe that Reed just needed the admiration, or that Reed hung around with him because, like others in the club, Devon usually went along with Reed's ideas. That wasn't necessarily true. Loyalty was important to all of them, but Devon had pride and would resent the others thinking he marched in lockstep with Reed. Devon could think for himself. It was just that Reed was a leader and Devon wasn't.

Once, when the two were alone in the clubhouse, Devon had come straight out and asked Reed what he saw in him.

39

In a rare moment Reed had been caught off guard, as if he'd never considered his friendships. Devon had felt hurt, and Reed, sensing it, had quickly apologized. To show his sincerity he'd confided in Devon things about himself—how after his mother had died he'd gotten into fights with his father, that he feared the idea of moving to still another town, that he worried his basketball skills wouldn't take him as far as he wanted. Devon had felt honored to be Reed's confidant. It was only that night that Devon realized Reed still hadn't asked anything about Devon Beaupre. What was the matter? Wasn't he interesting enough to Reed? Didn't he have something unique or valuable to offer the friendship? Maybe he needed to pass some test.

After an hour of hiking Devon reached a jagged slab of granite that soared skyward like a billowy sail. Reed had mentioned the rockface last night, had said that for a nontechnical climb it was difficult and challenging. The smooth, curved face was like a watch crystal and had few handholds or toeholds. So climb it, make something of yourself, show Reed, a voice ordered. Devon glanced to the path of rock cairns he'd left coming from the cabin. Remembering his first night in the mountains, he didn't want to get lost again.

The sun drifted obligingly behind a cloud bank, reducing the glare, as he began his ascent. Still, after a few minutes he was sweating heavily. Turning his shirt into a headband, Devon inched up, feeling for handholds while his boots squeaked against the rock. He traveled at a consistent pace, gaining some confidence as his nerves settled. He wished Reed were around. His foot levered toward a ledge when his heel suddenly chipped a rock loose. Devon watched the renegade stone clatter gracefully down.

His eyes traveled on into the valley. What they saw dismayed him. Two state forest rangers were crisscrossing the tall, waving grass. It would be only a minute before they raised their glances. Devon had seen search parties often enough. Every summer, rangers brought back into Olancha dozens of dehydrated campers or lost hunters. The rangers always carried backpacks, walkie-talkies, first-aid kits. Devon had no doubt whom this party was after.

Cold sweat glided down his ribs as he tried to think. His first decision was that he mustn't be seen. Beneath the feeling of satisfaction that the club was important enough to warrant a search effort, he was appalled by the idea of being discovered. Rangers were no more welcome at the club than were parents. His second decision was that he had to get down, quickly, and warn the others.

Devon lowered one foot, his toe wavering blindly in search of a hold. Position secured, the other foot dipped down. He began to move more rapidly, making a game out of danger. He was almost to safety when his right hand slipped. He teetered inward, then felt his body sway back and out. And then he was floating. He tucked his body in helplessly. Arms around his head, fetal position, eyes pinched shut. A scream bunched in his throat. The impact of the first boulder was buffeted by the fat and muscle of his shoulder, the second by his buttocks. He began to roll, spinning crazily, out of control. He expected to slam against an upright boulder, but his path stayed clear.

When he came to a stop, blood was dripping from his nose. He tried to pull himself up but couldn't. Was something broken? There was no acute pain, and he kept telling himself he was all right, that he had to get to the others. He'd only fallen about forty feet. Still, everything inside him quaked, buzzed, vibrated.

On his back he tried to breathe evenly. He waited for the rushing feet of the rangers, but there was only the wind soughing through the grass. He couldn't believe his fall hadn't been spotted. Luck—or was it? What if he were seriously hurt? As his shock ebbed, pain spiraled through his ribs.

Stupid, that's what you are, he thought as he lay very still. Not telling anybody, taking this needless risk. And what had he proved by the climb? Had he expected to instantly transform himself into another Reed? Was that who he really wanted to be? Was impressing somebody, even your best friend, worth anything at all? All he'd proven was that his thinking was fuzzy, that he didn't really know himself or what he wanted. He knew, too, he had another challenge now. For his thoughtless action he owed something to the club. If the rangers stumbled on him, fine, but he wasn't going to wave any white flag, no matter how scared he was. This was one test he was determined to pass.

The sweat on his face and shoulders began to cool. His watch had been smashed—the hands frozen at twenty-three past two—and it bothered him that he couldn't know the time. His earlier feelings about deadlines and appointments aside, he wanted to be sure of something. He listened for the rangers. Maybe they'd wandered in the other direction. When he finally got himself to a sitting position, everything was spinning. He made out a beige tent a few hundred yards away. The rangers were building a fire, bivouacking for the night. Devon dropped back in the grass and waited. Thirsty. Would Reed or the others try to find him? What if nightfall came first? How cold would it get? Would he freeze without a sleeping bag?

Doubts came and went. Maybe Reed wouldn't even come looking. How loyal a friend was he in a pinch? That had never been tested in the club. Standing together was easy when you had a common enemy, but when something happened within your ranks—

Ants crawled up his arm. Growing colder, he untied his T-shirt from his head and managed to pull it on. His eyes closed. Drifting.

Something warm touched his forehead.

"What?" he yelled, frightened. He tried to focus. The sky was coal gray and still spinning. The soothing hand touched him again.

"Are you all right?"

He made out Reed's face, the intense brown eyes now calm, concerned. "Oh, man," sighed Devon, "am I glad—"

"What happened?"

"—climbing that rockface." He felt incredibly stupid again. "I fell . . ."

Reed's fingers carefully probed his joints and bones. Devon winced when Reed touched his side. "I think you might have busted a rib or two. We'd better get home and get you to a doctor—"

"No," Devon said firmly. "I'll be all right. Help me up."

Reed looped Devon's hand around his shoulder and

pulled him up effortlessly. He'd forgotten how strong Reed was.

"Park rangers over there. They didn't see me." Devon went to point, but it hurt to raise his arm. Still, he could walk okay. He would survive without a doctor.

"Are you sure you're all right?"

"You've got some tape in your first-aid kit, don't you? Just bandage my ribs when we get back. I'll be fine." Reed still looked dubious. "Hey, I'm sure."

"Okay."

"How did you find me, anyway?"

"I started thinking where you might have gone. Last night your eyes lit up when I mentioned the rockface. And then I found your cairns. Smart of you, Devon. When I spotted the rangers I thought they might have found you."

"No way," Devon said proudly. He thought how quick and clever Reed had been to track him. He wondered again if he could ever be Reed's equal.

It was dark when they started for the cabin, Reed's flashlight dancing over the scrub and rock. After a while every step was jarring. Devon was sure he'd at least bruised some ribs. He refused to complain. All he could think about was how he'd screwed up. He felt even worse for doubting that Reed would come to save him. In a mutual test of friendship, Reed had passed, Devon flunked, gloriously.

"You sure those ribs are all right?" Reed broke the silence.

"I told you, I'm fine."

"Okay. I just wanted to be sure," he said, and, almost

as an afterthought, he added, "because we can't stay in our cabin anymore."

I understand, Devon was about to say, but he didn't. "What do you mean?"

"Those rangers will find us by tomorrow. I don't want that, do you? We've had enough of adults invading our privacy."

Devon nodded.

"We'll have to move on," Reed continued. "It's either go back to town or go somewhere else."

"Somewhere else?"

"Farther into the Adirondacks."

Devon had always known of the possibility of rangers finding them, and then the club would have to return to Olancha, but he'd never thought of another scenario. "Where would we go? Is there another cabin somewhere?"

"Maybe. I don't know. We've got tools to make a lean-to, if we have to. You've seen how well we work together. Hey, you organized us."

"How long would we stay?"

"Until we're good and ready to go back. You don't want any ranger or parent telling us when we have to—"

"No," Devon said automatically, but he wasn't sure how the others would react. Hadn't the understanding been they'd go back soon, anyway? They'd already been gone a week. "Wouldn't it be just as smart to head home now? Why keep running?"

"We're not running. We're here because we want to be. I'm not ready to go back," Reed said firmly. "Are you?"

Olancha could wait a while, Devon supposed, but they were getting low on food, and wouldn't the rangers pick up their trail? Reed was so confident that he didn't see any problems.

"We'll have to vote, of course," Reed said. "Tonight, after dinner. There'll probably be resistance. The others will raise the same questions you did." He looked at Devon. "I'll have to do a lot of talking. It would help me if you were on my side."

Devon didn't try to avoid Reed's glance. Reed had saved him today. Reed was aware of the debt, too. "Don't worry," Devon promised as they weaved through the scrub, his voice carrying over the symphony of cicadas, "I'll back you up all the way."

6

"Otis?"

"Yes."

"Benjy."

"What's a few more days? I'll deal with my dad when the time comes."

"Devon?"

"Let's hike on."

"Amber?"

Reed leaned toward the ribbons of orange and blue flame and glanced at the faces around the fire. Some looked tired, others uneasy. The day had been long, and though everyone was relieved Devon had been found in one piece, they were anxious about the rangers finding the cabin. Still, Reed's idea of hiking on had met more resistance than he'd expected. He didn't understand. It wasn't like they were moving to Yugoslavia. Making a game of avoiding the world was a way to make you feel alive. You had to decide who you wanted to please—yourself or your parents.

"Amber?" Reed called again.

"No," she said after a beat. Amber's eyes roamed to her sister. "Jade and I have to go back."

"Why?"

"Because we weren't supposed to be here in the first place."

A silence dropped over the group. Reed couldn't believe what Amber had said.

"Come again?" Reed demanded. "You had permission—"

"I'm sorry," Amber whispered, dropping her head. "It was okay with Mom, and we tried to convince Dad, but in the end he said no. Early in the morning we left anyway. We didn't want to miss out, or let everybody down. . . ."

"You go back if you want," Jade announced to her sister. "I'm not. *Nooooooo* way. We're just going to get punished—royally."

"We'd better get home and you know it."

Jade wagged her head. "I'm staying in the mountains."

"It's only going to be worse if we delay it."

"Look, I don't see a problem," Reed interrupted, his calm voice bringing the girls' attention back to him. "Stay a few more days. I'll speak to your father when we get back. Let him get angry at me. I'll tell him it was my idea." Reed remembered hiding under their window when his nerves had turned to jelly, but that had been an exception. He could handle Mr. Sheedy next time. He was sure.

"I have to agree with Amber," Marcy spoke up before

the twins could decide. "I want to go back, too. It's been a great trip, but sooner or later even good things have to end."

Reed pushed his stockinged feet closer to the fire. The air had a bite, and he thought of slipping on his parka. He already knew Marcy's arguments, they all did. Devon might be more hurt than he thought; staying in the mountains without a clear destination was risky; she didn't want to disappoint her parents further. Reed met Marcy's eyes. He could keep arguing but what was the point? Maybe Marcy and Amber would never understand what made this trip special.

"Okay, then, I guess that's it," Reed announced without a fight. "We don't have a unanimous vote about staying. That means we head back tomorrow."

Devon looked surprised, so did Benjy and Otis. No one had expected Reed to surrender so easily. The truth was, he felt tired of assuming responsibility. He did it all the time with the club, but he wondered if the others appreciated him enough. What good was being a leader if your followers weren't loyal? If Marcy and the others didn't trust his judgment, he wasn't about to force his will.

"Really? You mean it?" Marcy said to Reed.

"Like you said, it's been a good trip."

The others moved haltingly toward the cabin. They were feeling mixed emotions, Reed saw, and a lot of uncertainty. Not just because the trip was ending, but because of what its ending meant. What were they going to do for a clubhouse in town? Going home was going to mean new problems.

"Please don't be mad at me." Marcy dropped beside Reed at the fire.

"Who's mad?"

"I didn't mean to ruin the trip for you. We can all come up again."

"It won't be the same. Doing something the first time is always better. There's a feeling of discovery, surprise . . ."

Marcy looped her arm through his. "Do you think I'm being selfish? I don't like disappointing you. No one in the club does."

"You want to get back. I understand."

"You must think it's easy for me to oppose you. It isn't. My emotions keep getting in the way."

Reed stirred, studying the pretty face in the night shadows.

"I've always felt something special for you," she admitted. "I've never been able to come out and say it. It's been easier just being friends with you."

Friends? Reed wondered. What kind of true friend would go against him in a crucial situation? Devon and Otis hadn't.

"Why don't you want to get involved with me?" she asked suddenly. "Is it you or me?"

"It's not you."

"Why don't I believe you?"

Reed wondered if Marcy's self-doubt was real. No, just a game, he thought. Still, he didn't feel like explaining himself. He wasn't comfortable being intimate with anybody. Yet getting involved with Marcy would be a cinch. She was bright, fun, pretty, and she had a great body. He pushed the hair from her eyes. Their kiss was warm and natural, just like at the pond. He really did feel something for her. He felt, too, Marcy beginning to take control of their relationship, of the situation. He pulled back.

"I don't understand you," she said with a sigh. "A lot of boys are crazy about me—"

"They should be."

"So why aren't you? I know you're not afraid to take chances. You do it all the time in fighting the town."

"Maybe I just don't fall in love easily."

"Make an effort," she teased. "Like you said, the first time is always the best."

"If we do get involved," Reed asked seriously, "doesn't everything change?"

Marcy smiled mischievously. Wait and see, she was saying.

Reed knew things would change for him. Getting involved didn't just mean more responsibility; it meant trust and dependence. In his cautious way after his mother had been killed, he'd kept an emotional distance from the world. Marcy wasn't totally right about him not being afraid to take chances. Being a leader was easy for him, because it covered up the isolation he felt. But falling in love, that was new territory. He didn't know if he could control feelings he'd never had before.

Marcy brushed her cheek against his. "What's going to happen with us?" she whispered.

He kissed her. Then again, and both knew it meant something. Maybe it isn't so bad losing control, Reed thought. He could see himself falling in love with Marcy. For a moment he felt happy about the mystery, and felt a rare peace with himself, as if his battles with the world no longer mattered. He didn't think about the others in the club or his rotten life at home or even his plans for the future. The new sensation was too special to let go of.

7

"I was up half the night thinking . . . it wasn't an easy decision . . . but maybe we shouldn't go home just yet. . . ."

In the lifting darkness Marcy's eyes fixed on the fiery glow above the eastern peaks. The sky was so gorgeous. Then she noticed disbelief on Amber's face. The others were still asleep.

"Marcy, you can't be serious! Last night you made it clear you wanted to go back. Even Reed accepted it. What's going on?"

Reed was what was going on, though Marcy wouldn't admit it to Amber or the others. Her feelings for Reed were special, private, and overwhelming. She'd finally gotten what she felt was a commitment from the most evasive boy she'd ever wanted. She felt secure and confident enough to give Reed something back, something he wanted. Besides, the mountains were fun, weren't they? A few more days didn't mean the end of Western civilization.

"Your mom's bound to be worried to death about you," Amber pointed out.

"I know. I'm trying not to feel too guilty. I'll have to explain when I get back, that's all."

"At least you get along with your parents. What about me and Jade? We *have* to get back. Don't you care about us?"

Marcy sighed. "Of course I care about you. We're all friends. It's just that your dad will be as furious about seven days as ten days. I have to do what's right for me, too."

"I think Reed got to you."

"What's that mean?" Marcy flicked her head back.

"You're not being objective. We all came on the trip with the idea of going back on a set day. It was Reed who started changing things. I don't think it's fair. Nobody is running away from home or anything. As rough as my dad can be sometimes, he's still my dad, and home is home. I want to go back."

"Amber, I am being objective. Maybe Reed has helped me in that. I love my family, but the fact is I'm too tied to them and the small-town mentality. Getting away like this and being independent is good."

"It sounds like you're still trying to convince yourself." Amber tossed a pebble disconsolately against a tree. "What about me? What am I going to do?"

"I'll make you a deal. We stay just three more days. That's it. Then we go home. Okay?"

"What if Reed doesn't agree?"

"He will. And if he doesn't, we'll go back anyway."

"Sure," Amber said, giving her friend a good look. "Part of me feels like taking Jade and leaving now."

"Come on, we're a club, a really unique family. We always do things together. Just three more days. I promise."

Over breakfast Marcy told the others her feelings had changed. There were surprised faces. Reed was particularly pleased. On a topographical map he pointed to some squiggly lines near the Adirondacks' tallest peaks. "I've never hiked as far as Arthur's Pass," he admitted, "but that's what makes this a challenge." On the map the area looked nearly inaccessible, steep, rugged terrain that future search parties would have trouble reaching.

Reed rose and began to dismantle their cabin improvements, starting with the shutters.

"What are you doing?" Devon asked, stunned. "All our work— "

"Yeah—" Otis wagged his head in disbelief.

"Can't leave any clues," Reed said, and with a pocket knife he scraped away the words NO ADULTS ALLOWED. "The rangers would pick up the scent. . . ."

It was a good point, Marcy conceded, though she felt a little sad as she helped to remove the door and hide it in the brush. If the rangers looked closely they would still see signs of recent occupation, but maybe they would hurry by, she thought. Backpacks were restuffed, the fire put out, and embers buried. Carefully they covered their tracks.

Single file they moved through low brush and scattered granite outcroppings.

After a few hours everyone but Reed was tired. The pace was faster than on their first leg from town, or maybe the grade was steeper. Something, Marcy thought. As eager as she was, the hike began to feel uncomfortable. The sun wasn't as punishing as the humidity. They were all soaked. Marcy's socks were thick with briers, and her hair was stringy and tangled. Reed hadn't stopped for many rests, just a few minutes here and there to glance through Devon's binoculars, looking for the rangers. Marcy kept one eye on Benjy and the twins. They were struggling, especially Benjy, who continually slipped on rocks and labored to keep up.

On the run, Marcy pulled the last half of a melted Hershey from her backpack. The end of the chocolate. The coffee had run out that morning. So what, she'd get by. Reed wouldn't say it but he didn't think she had much discipline. Maybe she *was* a little spoiled. For being stuck in a backwater town, her family made things pretty nice for her. Marcy complained about the local injustices as loudly as anyone, but it always sounded slightly hollow because she didn't suffer as much as the others. She cared, she empathized, but the fact was, her life was pretty privileged. A little hardship in the mountains wouldn't be bad.

It was late afternoon when they reached Arthur's Pass. Marcy dropped wearily with the others in the barren hollow of low scrub and spindly trees. She rubbed the cramps from her legs, then angled her canteen to let the last warm drops fall on her tongue. Home, she thought, if you could call it that. She forced a laugh. The gray, solemn peaks still above them loomed like impassable walls. The setting was in sharp contrast to the flowering meadow and fragrant forests surrounding the cabin. End of the trail, no escape. Marcy wondered who Arthur might have been—a loony or masochistic explorer?

The hilly ground was studded with rocks, but Reed found a small clearing for their sleeping bags. The sky was overcast. With a wink Reed promised there'd be no rain that night. He was in good spirits, Marcy saw. No rangers had been spotted on the way, and now they were well camouflaged by a ridge separating them from the lower valley. "The perfect hideout," Reed said. Devon and Otis made a fire while Reed promised to find food. The map showed a vein of a river not too far away. Hungry stomachs were banking on trout. Marcy wanted to ask Reed if he needed company, but she decided there would be plenty of time together later.

Reed marched along the river bank and finally pulled his line from the water. A couple of thin, teasing shadows had darted under the current, but no fish had volunteered to become their dinner. Undaunted, Reed headed west toward a slope of stunted pines. In the waist of his jeans was his .45. For distance accuracy he wished he'd brought along a rifle, even a simple .22, but his father would have missed that more readily, and a rifle would have been awkward on a trek. What the hell, he liked the challenge of bagging a rabbit with a .45. He had seen evidence of warrens, and dusk was a time rabbits liked to forage. He had a sporting chance. Wouldn't everyone be pleased! He was the leader here and he would be the provider.

On a smooth boulder in the middle of the field he lay flat with the gun in his hands, scanning the brush. Luck never hurt, he thought, when two long, gray ears suddenly peeked above the shrub. Reed's stare followed the rabbit as it hopped toward a berry bush. His prey was a good thirty yards away, but Reed aligned his eye along the cold metal sight. With a shift in wind, the rabbit perked its nose up. Reed froze, watching back, thinking of the rabbit's innocence and beauty. Hard to kill. But he was becoming sentimental.

His finger squeezed the trigger. The bullet tore into the soft neck and spun the rabbit around like a top. The exit wound was the size of a silver dollar, Reed saw from his perch. On the ground, like someone stirring in his sleep, the rabbit twitched gently.

Reed gave a little yell of victory.

He ran over, tied the back legs of the animal together with fishing line, and hoisted his kill over his shoulder. He couldn't remember the last time he'd eaten rabbit in the mountains, but the meat had been tasty. The others were in for a treat. Reed lingered in the field, hoping for another kill, but his luck was gone for the day.

The sky turned leaden as he headed back over a ridge of shiny granite. At the next gorge, his boots scraping against the rock, he jerked his head around. There had been an echo to his steps, he was sure. His eyes darted from rock to rock. Spotting nothing, he kept moving. After a minute he dropped behind a crevice and waited.

The clear squeak of boots now. Whoever's following

knows how to track, Reed thought. Then he glanced at the rabbit over his shoulder. Blood dripped from the open neck. Pulling off his T-shirt, Reed wrapped it tightly around the carcass and tucked the bundle under his arm. His heart began to pump as he stole quickly in a different direction.

From behind a pyramid of pale oval rocks he spied back. A hundred yards down, Reed saw the mountain man on his haunches. His long braid reached to his shoulder blades. From Devon's description Reed knew it had to be the same guy. Reed gave the loner credit—he was a diligent hunter, and he covered a lot of territory—but why was hc following Reed? The crucial thing was not to lead him to their camp.

Taking a circuitous route, Reed passed through a cluster of spruces and white pines and found himself staring at a log cabin. Smoke funneled lazily from the chimney. He thought only a moment. With a grin he untied his stained shirt. Shaking the rabbit as he walked, he ran the trail of blood to the cabin door. Maybe it was a little dangerous to fool with the unknown, but he couldn't resist turning the tables on the mountain man. Call it a little joke, he thought to himself. He smiled as he remembered the fish he'd put in Brewster's locker. This was another challenge, and he had to try it.

On the porch he rewrapped the rabbit in his shirt and was set to run. Darkness was closing over the peaks without the customary fiery sunset. A metallic click broke the stillness. Reed's head swung up. Fifty yards away, shoulders pitched forward, the mountain man and his shotgun made an angry silhouette.

Reed's heart pushed to his throat. Run, he thought.

One leg made a feeble effort, but the other wouldn't follow. He remembered being under Mr. Sheedy's window. His stomach softened as he focused helplessly on the hunter. Like I'm the rabbit now, he thought. Then: run.

The shotgun blast exploded against the quiet sky. He tumbled down the porch stairs, the rabbit spilling from his arms. Somehow he picked himself up and spurted ahead, out of control, into the sanctuary of darkness.

8

"**Y**ou were getting too close to the guy's cabin. That's why he followed you," Devon volunteered the next morning. "When he saw you on the porch he took a couple of shots, aiming over your head. Just to scare you off. What did you expect—an invitation to dinner?"

The others joined in Devon's laughter. Reed forced a smile but he didn't agree. The mountain man was trouble, someone to avoid, just like he'd always said. Shaken by last night, Reed had considered moving camp farther west, only he didn't like running or being intimidated. He was fed up with any feelings of cowardice.

"Hey, we're on top of the world here," Otis interrupted as he took in a view of rolling, forested hills. "I hereby declare a new and sovereign state—Goof-Off Land!"

"I say we get to work," Reed spoke up.

Benjy grimaced. "What for? What's making us?"

"It's going to rain this afternoon."

Benjy studied the white fleecy clouds. "No way."

"Better to be prepared," Reed replied. "We can make a lean-to in half a day and be done with worrying. Sooner or later you need shelter."

"Reed's right," seconded Marcy.

"Don't be a killjoy," Amber said. "Everybody's bushed from yesterday. This isn't like home where we have chores. That's one reason I'm up here. . . ."

"So anybody for baseball?" Otis sang. With his boot heel he marked off a playing diamond in the sloping hollow, then gathered pine boughs for the bases. A thick, longish branch became a bat, a pinecone the ball. Reed, resigned to the mutiny, trotted on the field with the others.

"Hey, *batta, batta, batta* . . ." mocked Benjy as he stood on the pitcher's mound. Otis was at the plate. With a big grin Benjy delivered the first pitch. Otis took a full cut and missed by a mile.

"Choke!" Jade yelled.

At the next pitch Otis gritted his teeth and swung even harder. The pine cone fragmented in midair over the pitcher's mound. Otis was circling the bases when Benjy picked up a piece of the cone and tagged him.

"You're out," Benjy said smugly.

"Bull. There's no ball left."

"I got a piece of it. You're out."

"Yeah, next batter," Devon agreed.

"Stay out of this, Devon. . . ."

"Look, Otis, you're out, period. Next batter."

Otis gave Devon a hard look. Then he shoved Benjy out of his path and continued rounding the bases. Benjy scooped up a rock. Reed couldn't believe it. His warning shout was too late. The missile clipped Otis on the ear.

"You little bastard—" Otis spun around and charged the smaller boy. "Stay out of this," he yelled when Reed tried to intercede.

There wasn't much I could do anyway, Reed thought, as the chase continued into the woods. He was dismayed. In town they'd played a hundred baseball games without a disagreement. Then he thought about everyone refusing to build the lean-to. The laziness was out of character. What was going on?

When Otis and Benjy had calmed down, Reed took his fishing line and disappeared with Marcy over the hill. Let the others mess around, he'd do the work. Somebody had to.

"I really like it up here," Marcy said when they reached the river, "even if it is a little barren."

"The farther I am from Olancha, the more I like it."

"I've noticed."

"You don't like solitude?"

"I don't know if I've ever enjoyed being totally by myself. I'm not like you. I need company—friends or family or somebody." She took Reed's hand. "What I like most about being here is the chance to know you."

"Yeah? What have you learned you didn't already know?"

"That you're really pretty distrustful."

"Really?"

"You expect people to trust you, but you don't trust them."

63

"And you do?"

"Trust you? Absolutely."

"Always and forever?" he asked with a wink.

Marcy thought he meant it. And that he needed people to trust and believe in him. Reed stood alone so much of the time. When they returned to Olancha things would be different. Her parents would hardly be thrilled when she announced that Reed was her new boyfriend, but that was because they didn't understand him. Reed was just different. He made up his own goals and didn't back down. Her parents, when they saw that, would end up respecting him, just as she did.

As Marcy watched Reed flick his fishing line in and out of the water, she suddenly wondered what *she* needed. Would a boy to fall in love with be enough? She wasn't one for worrying about the future. She preferred just enjoying friends, school, the club, and letting things take care of themselves. Sometimes she felt guilty for not having more ambition. She wanted to make cheerleader next year, but if she didn't, she wouldn't get hysterical. She liked boys, clothes, experimenting with her hairstyle, rock music, movies—maybe her interests would always be average. What was wrong with just being content with yourself? The truth was, she wasn't counting on great things happening to her. Things might happen for Reed or Devon, but not everyone had the potential to be a first-rate athlete or writer. She was surprised now when she realized that even in her fantasies she didn't crave some extraordinary life. She knew she needed more independence, more responsibility, yet she was only comfortable with so many challenges. When things got too difficult, she was afraid she'd disappoint herself and others. She liked things easy, but that had limitations. She hadn't really considered all this before, and didn't know if she liked the new awareness.

"How about a turn?" Marcy asked, breaking away from her thoughts and coming behind Reed. "Give me the line."

"You think you'll have better luck?"

"I'm a lucky person. When I want something, I usually get it."

After a few minutes Marcy landed several brown trout, though hardly trophy size. She and Reed scampered back to camp as a drizzle began. Reed deboned and cooked the fish. The others hung impatiently under an overhang. Everybody was starved. After lunch Reed mentioned the lean-to again.

"It's going to pour by evening," Marcy backed him up.

"All right," Devon conceded. "Maybe we should get on it."

Amber looked skeptical. "How do you know it's going to rain? There's a good breeze—maybe the clouds will blow away."

"Can't it wait, Reed?" Otis joined in.

Reed shook his head in disappointment. If they didn't want to help, fine. He seized the ax and headed alone to a thicket of pines. He had seen storms strike without warning in the Adirondacks, felt temperatures drop twenty degrees in as many minutes. It was no fun to be without shelter then. He shinned up the first tree and took several whacks just as the thunder pealed. Terrific, he thought, trying to work faster. After a minute it was as if the sky was one giant spigot.

"Reed, come down, you can't work in this," Marcy called.

He only relented when lightning began to blaze around him. Joining the others under the overhang he watched the sky darken and rumble. If only I'd insisted and they'd built the lean-to this morning, he thought.

For five hours they huddled together. The rain pinged against rocks and made puddles by their feet. Around dusk the storm broke up, allowing them to forage for food, but before they could prepare it, the rain resumed. Amber and Jade hadn't brought heavier clothes with them. When they began to shiver, Reed handed them his blanket and went back to watching the sky. No one had anything to say.

By evening the whine of mosquitoes filled the air. Half-damp sleeping bags were squeezed together under the narrow overhang. The wind gusted into their faces, bringing more rain. Reed used a tarp to deflect the onslaught and nestled farther into his bag. He tried not to think of his hunger. All he could hope was that the sky would clear by morning.

9

The storm lasted thirty six hours. Prisoners under the overhang, they filled the time with word games and stories and quick forays for berries and wild onions. Everyone was cold and hungry. The only good thing, thought Reed, was that no search team would venture out in this weather. When the rain finally stopped, Reed knew they'd be okay—if they acted quickly. Fresh clouds were already hovering on the sky's edge like angry ships massing for war.

"Let's get that lean-to built," he spoke up, running a hand over the stubble on his chin.

Hard stares shot back at him, as if he were to blame for bringing everybody to such a forsaken spot. He couldn't believe their fickleness. It wasn't his fault it had rained, was it? Had everybody forgotten the reasons for the hike? Hadn't there been a vote? They'd been unanimous in wanting to come, he hadn't ordered them.

"How much longer are we going to stay?" Amber asked moodily, not for the first time.

"We'll see."

"I don't know what difference a shelter will make. Unless you can install a clothes dryer and a bathtub." She scratched an arm reddened by mosquito bites.

"Give Reed a chance," Devon said.

"I've been thinking a lot about going home," Amber continued. "I mean, we've been away eleven days. Don't look so surprised, Reed. I know—I've counted them. And it feels like twenty. This just isn't fun anymore." Her glance jumped to Marcy. "Remember what you promised me about heading back?"

Marcy's face flushed and she looked away.

"If we'd built the lean-to when I suggested it, you wouldn't feel this way," Reed interrupted. He couldn't stand Amber's hypocrisy. "You're a quitter."

"I am not. I'm being reasonable. *You're* acting like a bully. You've been forcing your will on us almost every step of this trip."

"No, he hasn't," Marcy said. "He's been the leader."

"Marcy," Amber broke in, "he's a dictator. All his new ideas aren't so great. He manipulates us. There may be a vote, but one way or another Reed gets his way. Or haven't you noticed? No one feels comfortable opposing him."

"Maybe it's uncomfortable for me putting up with you," Reed answered coolly.

Amber threw her hands up at the obvious. "Then why don't you just let us go back to town?"

"Because I don't think you're giving the mountains a fair chance. And I still don't see what's waiting for us in Olancha. Anyway, you make it sound like you're being held prisoner. You're not."

"Reed, let's face it," Otis said more calmly, trying to he a peacemaker, "the days are getting pretty long up here."

"It'll get better once the rain stops."

"I know, but I promised my brother I'd get back to work sooner or later."

"Maybe the rain's never going to stop," Benjy said with a worried glance at the sky.

Reed turned without a word, grabbed the ax, and marched to a bevy of pines. He could understand Benjy caving in—he was the youngest—but Otis? What had happened to his good friend, the friend he'd given up his basketball for when he was facing the sheriff? All the bitching and bickering—it didn't feel like the club he cared about. What about the ideal of sticking together, sticking it out? Was the club only good when things were easy? He'd thought he could count on the others. He knew they could always count on him.

Reed clambered up the first tree and began hacking furiously at the limbs. He would show everybody what could be done if you were determined. As limbs were dropped, Devon and Marcy broke off the useless branches. Benjy and Otis came to help, but Amber and Jade sat sullenly under the overhang and took turns combing each other's hair. Didn't they care at all? By midmorning the sky began to rumble again. The rain started as a drizzle, grew more steady, and finally came down in sheets. Reed refused to stop. By noon he had cut sixty good-sized pieces.

Cold and exhausted, after lunch he lashed together the limbs with heavy twine into three separate, equal-sized partitions about ten feet in length. In one he hacked out a small opening for an entrance. With Devon and Otis's help, the partitions were laid in place against a vertical rock face, tied together at the joints, and the earth sloped away from the bottom for drainage. Quarters would be cramped, but seven sleeping bags could fit.

"It looks great," Marcy said, standing by Reed as they examined the structure.

"Part of me had doubts," Devon admitted, "but here she stands. . . ."

Reed thought everyone felt better. He knew he did. The lean-to wasn't a world-class hotel, but it was something to be proud of, maybe even more than their first cabin. To finally accomplish something after all the restless waiting . . . "Let's get a roof on," he said.

"I'll cut the extra limbs," Otis volunteered. Reed watched him saunter back to the trees with the ax. Turning, Reed gave Amber and Jade a wave, wanting to patch things up. Then he heard the shrill cry.

"Damn handle slipped," Otis said angrily, clenching his teeth, as Reed and the others hurried over. A deep gouge between his thumb and forefinger spurted blood. Reed used his bandana to stanch the flow.

Reed heard the twins whispering behind him. Were they blaming him for this, too? If he'd just been sensible and agreed to turn back, he imagined them saying, this would never have happened. They were afraid to speak to him directly. Otis's hand needed sutures, but what could anyone do up here? Reed was sorry his first-aid kit had been almost depleted. He'd been responsible in planning this trip and in taking precautions—but some things you couldn't anticipate.

"Do you want to go home?" Reed turned patiently to Otis. His friend looked white. "Just tell me—"

"I don't feel too great," he managed. "Let's see in the morning. Devon's bruised body is doing okay, maybe I'll be fine, too."

"Whatever you want to do is okay. The rest of us will follow."

Reed wanted to show Amber and everybody he was no bully. He and Devon moved back to the trees to finish Otis's work. The others carried sleeping bags into the shelter and began scavenging for food. Reed realized he'd learned something on this trip. Friends that you thought you knew could surprise and disappoint you. He'd thought the members of the club were different. Why should they be? Maybe he had expected too much, or maybe his ideals were too high for them. He tried to forget his disappointments by thinking of college. And of his basketball future. In college things would be different. He'd hang onto old friendships from Olancha—Devon would be loyal, Otis, too, and Marcy, he hoped—but change wouldn't be a bad thing.

10

Light filtered between the pine limbs of the lean-to. As he stirred awake Reed saw the shallow pools around his sleeping bag. He couldn't believe his roof had leaked, or that he hadn't wakened sooner. The others were already up, except for Otis, who tossed fitfully in his bag. "How do you feel?" Reed asked.

"Lousy," he moaned.

Reed touched his friend's forehead. The bandana on Otis's hand had come loose, and dirt had gotten in. The red, puffy flesh alarmed Reed. If he hadn't been so exhausted the night before he might have checked the bandana. "I'm going to fix you some burdock to give you strength. Its roots have a lot of carbohydrates."

Reed found Devon and Benjy squatting by the fire. Neither looked happy.

"Marcy went fishing," Devon answered Reed's inquiring look, "else there's no breakfast." Devon tried not to sound too down. Reed was doing his best under the circumstances, better no doubt than Devon could do, but the fact was, everyone was miserable. Things would have been better had they stayed in their first cabin. Devon realized he'd gone along with Reed's idea to move here. He'd stuck with his friend's choices since, but now it was time to head home. His aching body was ready for a hot bath. Maybe he'd even have a doctor check him out.

"Where're Amber and Jade?" Reed asked, looking around.

"I guess on a walk. They were already gone when I got up. Have you looked at Otis?"

"He's feverish," Reed said, a little defensively, as he grabbed the shovel and drifted toward a cluster of burdock. Look, I do my best, he wanted to tell Devon. I do more for you guys than you ever do for me. So why do I get blamed when the smallest thing goes wrong? When Reed had dug up the tough, starchy tubers, he boiled them for easier digestion and threw in the cut-up stems. There were other edible plants around, though some tasted pretty bitter. In a pinch anyone who knew something about the wilderness could survive. As Reed headed to the lean-to he noticed the twins' backpacks and sleeping bags were already tied up—was that a hint?

Marcy finally returned but without any fish. Reed saw the looks of disappointment. He was hungry, too.

"Can we pull out of here now?" Devon looked at Reed. "We can find food on our way down."

Reed nodded solemnly, surrendering. "Okay. I don't

think we have a chance. We'll split as soon as Amber and Jade get back.''

He saw that Devon was relieved. Reed started to pack his gear when he felt Marcy staring at him.

"Reed, there's something you should know," she said.

He listened to her anxious tone. He didn't want more surprises. Was she turning against him, too? He was suddenly afraid the relationship he wanted with Marcy would be over before it began.

"What's up?" He tried to sound casual.

"I don't know this for sure, so maybe it's wrong to start worrying. But last night I heard the twins whispering. This morning they got up really early. No one's seen them since." She hesitated. "Maybe they left for home."

Reed tried not to show his surprise. He'd known all along how unhappy Amber and Jade were. They'd been too chicken to confront him about their leaving Olancha without their father's permission—how could he expect them to level about this? Yet he was surprised, or maybe just hurt. Didn't they trust his leadership at all? Or realize he cared enough about Otis's being hurt that they'd all go home now? What about club rules? There was supposed to be a vote.

"They left without their backpacks?" he asked, incredulous.

"Maybe they didn't want us to become suspicious and go after them. Please don't be too angry."

"I'd like to know how they're getting home. I've got the only compass. It's over twenty-four miles to Olancha. They can't make it in a day—"

Marcy felt awful. She might have discouraged Amber

74

and Jade when she'd heard them whispering last night. Somehow she'd hoped things would just work out by themselves. That was usually her response to trouble. "Amber must have the confidence to think she can reach the cabin by night," Marcy volunteered, "then hike to town in the morning."

Confidence doesn't mean much without experience, Reed thought. Amber was no more used to the mountains than was Benjy. The odds were she and Jade would take a wrong turn and get lost. He didn't want to face Mr. Sheedy if that happened. But Reed was determined to find the girls without being prodded by fear of their father. Coming up here had been his idea. He was still in charge, even if not everybody acknowledged that.

Reed hitched his canteen to his belt and grabbed the binoculars. "I can't get Otis home while I'm worrying about Amber and Jade. We all have to go back together."

"But what if you can't find them?" Marcy said. "Or if it takes longer than you think?"

"I have to try."

"Are you sure?"

"Don't you feel responsible for them?"

"Of course, and I feel badly for not stopping them, but they left on their own. They took that chance. I'm worrying about Otis now."

"I'm a good tracker. I'll be back by noon," Reed promised. "Trust me. Just stay put till then. Tell the others I'll be back."

She gave him a kiss. "I trust you, Reed. I'll tell everybody." She didn't like this tension. For a moment she worried about facing her parents tomorrow. That was going

75

to be more than unpleasant. All she wanted was to be with Reed, she thought, watching as he disappeared over a hill. She didn't want Devon, Otis, and Benjy to know how much she cared for him. Not yet. She just hoped Reed came back with the twins and everybody got home safely.

Reed scampered over the boulders, taking chances with his footing. His imagination moved even faster. What time had Amber and Jade left? How far could they have traveled? His glance fell to his compass every few minutes, but he remembered the route well enough. He hoped the twins did, too. He was relieved that the ground was still moist from the rains and he could pick up occasional prints. As the terrain turned more rocky the prints vanished. Every few minutes he swept his binoculars over the harsh landscape. He tried to anticipate—if they did veer off course—where the girls might make their mistake. The first forest was straight ahead—would they plunge through it or try a detour? Reed elected to move around it.

By noon he began to worry. He was two hours out of camp and hadn't any clue to the girls' whereabouts. He was worried about Otis, too. As the sun beat down he cupped his hands around his mouth. The twins' names echoed over the mountains. If they hear me they'll respond, he thought. But all Reed heard was the incomprehensible chatter of a blue jay.

He drank from his canteen and began to backtrack, slowing his pace as his eyes swept more carefully over the landscape. In a stretch of grassy meadow he found more prints, then part of a shoelace with hearts from Amber's sneakers. The girls were straying east, confusing this meadow for the one near the cabin. Reed hurried on. An hour later, edging toward a forest of tall spruces and hemlocks, he watched the sun glint off what he thought might be a rifle barrel. He jerked up the binoculars. Through a maze of speckled boulders a slight, dark figure loped uneasily, as if knowing she was lost, her hair clip shooting back the sun like a mirror.

"AMBER!" Reed roared.

A few hundred yards ahead the girl turned with a start. Reed focused on Jade, too, edging out from behind a boulder like her sister's shadow.

He waved anxiously and called again. They stared for the longest of moments, as if they didn't recognize Reed, or couldn't believe he had come after them.

"Leave us alone!" came Amber's thin but defiant voice.

"IT'S ME—REED!" he shouted, in case there was any confusion. "YOU'RE GOING THE WRONG WAY! COME BACK! WE'RE ALL GOING HOME TOGETHER! OTIS, TOO!"

"No!"

"WHAT ARE YOU TALKING ABOUT!"

They studied him for another moment, squinting out the sun, absolutely still.

Then they turned and started running.

11

"**M**arcy, what time is it?"
Devon studied the fractured crystal of his watch with frustration.

"You just asked me a minute ago. Almost five."

Devon arched his neck to the blackening sky. He gave their luck another hour, then it would pour buckets. Otis was in a feverish sleep. Benjy sat sullenly against the lean-to, whittling with a dull knife, keeping to himself just like the twins had. Was he thinking of going back on his own, too? Devon didn't have to ask Marcy what she wanted. "Wait for Reed," she'd told him, "he can't be gone much longer." Devon wasn't sure. Reed wasn't perfect. Maybe the twins had eluded him, or he'd gotten lost, or run into trouble. The tension Devon felt was awful. He felt the same way when he read mystery novels. Only now he couldn't turn to the last page. He hadn't thought about writing almost the entire time they'd been away. There certainly was something to record about this trip, but he wasn't sure what he'd say.

Devon rose light-headedly and climbed the rocks behind the lean-to. He could see for almost half a mile—no trace of Reed or the twins. His eyes came to rest on a distant haze of smoke.

"I've got an idea," he said when he rejoined the others. Benjy didn't pay attention. Marcy cocked her head suspiciously, as if she thought Devon was making trouble. He resented that. Somebody had to take charge. By showing some independence and concern Devon hardly considered himself being disloyal to Reed—and as for club rules, well, things were different now.

"What's your idea?" Marcy said.

"We have to do something—get food, antibiotics for Otis—"

"Sure, just walk to a drugstore."

Devon and Marcy had a casual, easygoing friendship, but then they'd never had much to disagree about. He had wondered before if Marcy had a thing for Reed, and on this trip he'd watched them definitely grow closer. Now he felt uncomfortable as they looked at one another. "I think I know where the mountain man's cabin is. I'm betting he's got food and medicine."

Marcy shook her head. "I promised Reed we'd stay put."

"How could this make him angry? We're just trying to do the right thing for Otis."

"I don't think Reed would like it."

"What if something's happened?" Devon argued.

"Nothing's happened. It just took Reed longer to find Amber and Jade. He'll be back."

"You don't know that."

"You don't know otherwise," she retorted.

Devon gave up. Marcy was in Reed's corner all the way. Still, Devon would do what he thought was right. Quietly, he left the lean-to and began hiking in the direction of the smoke. After twenty minutes he crossed a rock-strewn meadow, glided down a knoll, and stared at the well-preserved wooden cabin set on a foundation of rocks. Reed might have doubts, but Devon was intrigued by someone living in isolation—without a town, friends, conveniences. Without all the dangers and corruption of civilization. Why did Reed automatically assume that the mountain man was trouble and that Devon's impressions were naive? They might be best friends, but he and Reed had some differences of opinion. Devon held out hope for the unknown while Reed treated it with suspicion. It was as if Reed thought anything he couldn't control was going to hurt him.

"Anybody home?" Devon shouted, approaching the cabin.

When there was no answer he called again. For a moment he thought of turning back, checking for Reed at camp, but the mountain man had left a fire going, so he couldn't be far away. Devon moved up the stairs. "Hello," he called, and pushed open the door. His eyes moved around the single large room with wide-planked floors. Neat and clean. A made bed, rifles stacked in a corner, wood-burning stove, an old porcelain sink. Freshly baked bread sat on the table. Devon felt his hunger again. The setup was primitive but sufficient. Devon didn't feel like a trespasser, more like an admiring visitor.

The door squeaked open behind him.

In the soft cabin light the stranger didn't look so fierce. He was in worn Army fatigues. There was a sadness or resignation in the bleached eyes and lined forehead. His broad shoulders and considerable height were imposing but not menacing. Devon waited for the man to speak, but when he didn't, Devon had no trouble talking himself.

"My friends and I need help," he began.

12

Reed watched as Amber and Jade threaded their way through the boulders, jerking their heads around to make sure he kept his distance. For a second his anger got the better of him. Abandon them, he thought, let them get lost. But he couldn't. If they kept going in the same direction they'd end up miles from streams or campers or any town. He shouted again. When they didn't stop he picked up his pace. They ran, too. He was only trying to save them, and this was their thanks?

He was surprised at what agile runners they were, and how much energy they had, as if they'd taken the rest breaks he'd never allowed for himself. Still, he was much stronger and faster, and after a few minutes, pinning them against a granite outcropping, he closed in.

He leaped from a final ledge. Somehow his foot, dragging, caught on the lip. He tried to straighten his leg but the ground rushed up too quickly and he crumpled. Pain whipped through his ankle. With a sharp cry he rolled on his back, furious at himself. As if the accident had never happened he jumped up and tried to run.

"Amber!" He was startled by his voice. He sounded weak and helpless. "Hey—I'm hurt!"

The pain forced him to a halt. He waited for their footsteps. Instead the wind churned around him in mockery. Hadn't they heard him? Or did they think this was a trick? With an effort Reed hobbled back to the ledge and boosted himself up, waving his hands over his head. Finally they glanced back. They stood together, deliberating. Couldn't they see him half bowed over? He warned them again of the wrong direction, and asked for help. Reed expected some recognition, a sense of loyalty that had to go deeper than their momentary panic. He could see their faces contort—was it confusion?—more fear? He couldn't believe it when they began running away from him again.

Reed slumped to the ground in disgust. Forget it, he thought. I've done everything I can for them. Mr. Sheedy would be raging furiously, but no one could logically blame Reed for whatever happened to the twins. He unlaced his boot. His ankle was red, tender, and still ballooning. Was it broken or just sprained? No matter, he should soak it in cold water. The closest river was back at camp. If he could stand the pain, and kept a steady pace, he might be there by early evening. In the next forest he found a sturdy limb to use as a walking stick.

After an hour he rested. When he tried to stand again his legs had turned to stone. The adrenaline that had carried him the first few miles was gone. He pushed ahead more tentatively. He thought of his bed at home, of a hot shower, of just lounging in the old clubhouse. The old club was a long way from what the club had become now.

The air grew cooler and the wind gusted, raising swirls of dust and bending the tops of lanky pines. Reed's entire leg began to throb. He could accept the pain, he would have to. Fighting it would be pointless, because it was part of him. By dusk he found the river where they'd fished, then the familiar landscape of spindly trees and low scrub. Just over the hill he'd be at camp.

He felt a little better. The air was magically clear and light. Any rain clouds had been chased away by the wind. Reed hoped that Otis and the others hadn't given up on him. Maybe things would be okay after all. He'd get some sleep, and they'd all leave first thing in the morning. He thought again of the twins. He was furious at them, but still he hoped they'd run into stray campers and be helped.

At the crown of the hill Reed eyed the cluster of bodies below. He used the binoculars to see that Otis had his hand out as he squatted against the lean-to. The mountain man was wrapping it with fresh dressing. Reed couldn't believe it. Hadn't Marcy promised to sit tight till he returned? Or maybe it was Devon who'd made contact with the loner. Didn't anybody remember how the guy had shot at Reed? How could they trust a stranger instead of waiting? Reed was livid. He'd been betrayed. Even though his legs and body ached, he sneaked down behind the lean-to and crawled toward his backpack.

13

"**G**et away!"

Devon's hands lurched. He didn't know whether he was more shocked to see Reed or the .45. And who was he pointing the gun at, anyway? "Reed, what are you doing—"

"Get away from him, Devon."

"Reed, this is Fletcher. He was a medic in Vietnam. There's no problem here—" The mountain man finished wrapping Otis's hand and looked at Reed with less than friendly eyes. "Reed, he brought us food and antibiotics."

"Fine, so now he can be on his way."

Devon watched as Marcy moved to Reed's side. Benjy and Otis looked confused. Devon tried to apologize to Fletcher, but the man saw he wasn't wanted and quietly left.

"Fletcher was being a Good Samaritan, and you treated him like he had the plague," Devon said angrily to Reed.

"And maybe when you weren't looking he'd grab your sleeping bags and gear as payment for his work. What do you know about him, anyway? Maybe he's been in trouble. Maybe he's hiding out here. Why did he shoot at me a couple of days ago?"

"The same reason you pulled a gun on him. He's suspicious by nature. Vietnam probably made him that way. What's your excuse for not trusting anybody but yourself?"

"I don't need one. I asked you guys to stay put. What kind of loyalty is that? And remember the rules about not allowing adults in?"

"Stop it, you two," Marcy said. She hated the fighting. Things were bad enough. The twins weren't back, and they were still a long way from home. Suddenly she noticed Reed was favoring one leg. "What happened?"

"I found Amber and Jade but they wouldn't stop for me. Not even when I sprained my ankle." Reed tucked the gun in his backpack and looked at everyone with disappointment. "I really can't believe it. Not just what Amber and Jade did, but everybody— We're a club—all for one, one for all—or we're supposed to be. For the last few days we've forgotten that. I want it to go back to the way it was."

Devon found Reed looking right at him. Devon nodded. Things really had gotten too crazy. He was sorry for jumping on Reed. Everyone was just frustrated. In the morning they'd all head to town, tell the rangers where to look for Amber and Jade, and settle up with their parents.

86

Eventually they'd find a new clubhouse and start over. Devon wanted to believe in the club and all that it stood for.

That evening Devon was the first in his sleeping bag. He slept heavily until early morning, when a deep, churning noise filled the air. His eyes shot open in fright. Was it a dream? When he listened again the noise was gone. He told the others about it over breakfast, but no one else had heard anything.

14

Reed rewrapped his bandana around his forehead and hobbled in pain through the low scrub. Marcy, Benjy, Otis, and Devon marched in a listless formation. Otis was definitely feeling better, Reed saw, but he would bet even without Fletcher's help Otis could have made this trip. It was Reed who found the hike strenuous. He'd spent a restless night. His ankle hadn't bothered him so much as his fears of Fletcher returning. In the morning he'd wedged the .45 in his belt, camouflaged by a long, loose-fitting T-shirt. In his tired condition his imagination and fears played on him, but why take chances? As the sun bounced off the surrounding rocks, the canopy of bleached sky shimmered and dipped. There was no breeze. Reed couldn't remember ever being so tired and unfocused. He couldn't wait till they reached the cabin and the swimming pond.

Near shade trees he waved for the others to stop. He wrestled out of his backpack and dropped in the grass. His eyes were half-closed. Just five minutes of rest, he thought. The leaves dappled the sun into a pleasing pattern. The others might have wanted to keep moving but he had to rest.

The next thing he knew he heard somebody call his name.

"What?" he answered foggily, annoyed, half in a dream. He was incapable of moving.

"Reed Higdon—"

Reed squirmed up. "What?"

"Get up."

He raised himself with difficulty. The voice didn't sound like Devon's. When Reed turned he saw the others looking behind him. He swung his head back. Twenty feet away on a boulder stood the twins' father, cradling a shotgun. He stared down at Reed.

"We're just on our way back," Reed said quickly, wondering if this was really happening. Where had Mr. Sheedy come from? Dropping on his haunches, Reed picked nervously at a tuft of grass. He hated the silence. Mr. Sheedy's wide, pockmarked face looked unforgiving. "What brings you up here?" Reed asked, trying to keep his voice steady.

"You kidnapped my girls."

Reed thought it was a joke. "I what?"

"Ranger helicopter found 'em this morning. That's how I got here. They were half-starved. Running from you."

Reed shook his head in wonder.

"You forced 'em on your trip. They had to escape. They told me everything."

"Mr. Sheedy, now look—"

"Come over here, Reed."

Reed had figured Amber and Jade would lie a little—but not like this. Were they that frightened of their father? Or just mad at Reed? He was shocked. Maybe Mr. Sheedy was no Einstein, but didn't he have any doubts about their story? After all, the twins talked to Mr. Sheedy about going on a hike. Didn't he ever consider that they would disobey him? Maybe not, Reed reconsidered.

"That's not the way it was at all," Reed answered, trying to defend himself. He was so tired that Mr. Sheedy's figure began to blur.

"You won't be scaring my girls anymore. Come over here."

Reed watched the shotgun. At least it hadn't left the crook of Mr. Sheedy's elbow. But why had he brought it along? Reed glanced at the others, who were not far away. They stood motionless, frightened. Reed's legs ached but he got up and stepped forward. He wouldn't be afraid. When he saw his hands shaking he stuffed them in his pockets.

"Look," he explained to Mr. Sheedy, "I admit that the trip was my idea. We needed another clubhouse. The town is tearing ours down. I knew of one up here. Amber and Jade told us you gave them permission to come with us. We stayed longer than planned. I take responsibility for that, but I didn't see any real harm . . ."

Reed saw that his speech wasn't registering. Mr. Sheedy's

face stayed rigid. Reed was grateful when Marcy verified his story. The others nodded along. Still, Mr. Sheedy wasn't buying. He looked as if he thought Reed had persuaded everybody to lie. Reed was amazed. He didn't lie to anybody, including Mr. Sheedy. He hated lies and deception. That's what the club fought against.

"Admit it. You took my daughters. You forced them to go with you."

"No," Reed said adamantly. "It was my idea to go, I admit that," he repeated, remembering his promise to the twins to stick up for them, "but there was never any force or threats. In the end they made up their own minds. When they panicked and ran away, I tried to stop them."

"Liar."

The anger swelled in Mr. Sheedy's voice and his face grew red. Reed's defiance was making things worse. Still, he refused to back down. It was a question of principle. Mr. Sheedy raised his shotgun.

"Come here, boy."

"What for?"

"Do as you're told—"

Reed took a couple of steps forward. He had no reason to run or hide or act like he'd done something terrible. Let Mr. Sheedy try to make him change his story. He wouldn't.

"I'm coming with you, Reed," Devon said in a loud voice, moving beside his friend. Marcy started to approach, too, but Reed waved her back. "Don't worry, he's only trying to scare us," Devon whispered to Reed.

"I just want Reed. Everyone else stay put," Mr. Sheedy ordered. Reluctantly, Devon came to a halt. "Boy, you've been making trouble in our town for too long," Mr.

Sheedy said when Reed stood only inches from his face. "No one's stopped you. That's made you act even bigger. Big to all your friends. Big to my girls. Now you've gone too far. . . ."

The shotgun barrel was pushed into Reed's ribs, nudging him ahead.

"What are you doing?" Reed demanded.

"Move."

"Where?"

The shotgun barrel jabbed him again. Mr. Sheedy turned to the others with a final warning to stay put. Then he and Reed stumbled around the boulders and kept walking, out of sight. Reed's heart began to race.

"Get on your knees," Mr. Sheedy said when they came to a clearing.

"What do you think you're doing?"

"I'm going to make you tell the truth—"

"I already did!" Mr. Sheedy pushed him to a crouching position until Reed's head touched his knees. Dust filled his nostrils. The .45 pressed uncomfortably into his stomach.

"You don't have to impress your friends anymore. It's just you and me."

"I've got nothing else to say." Reed heard the shotgun hammer click into place. He couldn't believe this. Was Mr. Sheedy just trying to scare him like Devon suggested, or was he really serious? There were no witnesses, Reed realized.

"TALK!"

Reed could feel the hot, angry breath on his neck. "No." His voice was a tremble.

"You got five seconds. . . ."

"I didn't do anything wrong! I told you everything! Amber and Jade are the liars!"

"Four—"

"Please!"

"Three."

He tried to struggle up. Mr. Sheedy kicked him in the ribs. "I didn't do anything!"

". . . two . . ."

Reed's head and stomach spun out of control. His whole body trembled. Mr. Sheedy was going to kill him. He knew it now. He had to do something. His adrenaline began to pump.

"Time's up—"

15

The blast rang in Devon's ears like some terrible nightmare. He looked at the others just as the second roar came. Lurching up, he didn't have time to be afraid. Marcy was behind him as he sprinted toward the spot where Reed and Mr. Sheedy had vanished.

In a clearing Devon stopped cold. Mr. Sheedy, arms contorted behind his back, was on his side, neck angled back unnaturally. The jagged hole in his throat was the size of a fist. His shirt was red and damp. The shotgun was at his side. Devon thought he'd be sick.

"He's dead," Reed mumbled, in shock himself. He sat a few yards from the body, hunched down, breathing rapidly.

"You wrestled the shotgun away?" Devon managed to

get the words out. He looked at Marcy. She closed her eyes.

"What?" said Reed.

"You shot him?"

Reed shook his head. "No. Someone else."

Devon didn't understand. Who else was there?

"I caught a glimpse of him. He had a shotgun, too. He was tall. I think it was Fletcher."

"Fletcher?" Devon's head jumped around. He didn't see anybody.

"Mr. Sheedy fired once, just away from my head, to scare me. . . . The second blast came from over there," Reed said, pointing to an outcropping twenty yards away.

Devon examined the spot where Reed said he had been forced to kneel. Maybe the birdshot from Mr. Sheedy's blast was buried in the soft dirt. It was hard to tell. The story sounded so wild, but Devon was reluctant to challenge his friend. Reed didn't lie. "Are you all right?" Devon asked.

Reed nodded numbly. Marcy walked over to comfort him. When Benjy and Otis approached they stared at the body. Devon told them what had happened.

"What do we do now?" Otis asked, turning white.

Marcy said automatically, "We have to go to Sheriff Covington. Or the state ranger office."

"It's pretty straightforward," Devon thought out loud, trying to push away his panic. "Mr. Sheedy held a rifle to Reed. Then he fired at him. If Fletcher hadn't been around, Reed might be dead. It was all justified."

"That's right," Benjy said. "Everyone knows Mr. Sheedy had a temper. And he was furious over Amber and Jade. We all heard that."

Reed pulled himself to his feet. He paced in front of the group. Finally he said, "No. We can't do it that way at all."

"What do you mean?" asked Devon.

"How can you be so naive? Tell Covington or the rangers? What do you think's going to happen?"

"Nothing bad," Otis guessed. "There're four of us to back you up."

"With the way Covington feels about me and our club, we're still going to get blamed. Correction, *I'm* going to get blamed. Mr. Sheedy was Covington's close friend. What chance do I stand? Where's Fletcher to back up *my* story? He'll never admit to shooting anyone, even if it was justified. The guy doesn't want trouble. That's why he's living out here, remember?"

"Wait a second," Devon stopped Reed. "Why are you so worried about Covington? This is state land. It's not his jurisdiction."

"Right," Marcy said.

Reed threw up his hands. "You don't think Covington won't get his nose in this when he learns I'm involved? He knows every ranger in this park. They're all buddies. He'll insist on working with them, steering them toward *his* conclusions. . . ."

"Then what about going to Hugo?" Devon asked. "He's a fair man. He'll understand. He wouldn't take the sheriff's word automatically."

"How do you know?" Reed pressed.

"Because I know Hugo."

"Too much of a risk," Reed judged. "Even if Hugo did take our side, he doesn't have any real influence."

Devon understood Reed's point, but it bothered him to have to lie. They were all innocent—why should they lie? Besides, he was terrible at deceiving, just not used to it, and what lie were they going to tell, anyway?

Reed unhitched the shovel from his backpack.

"What are you doing?" Devon said, feeling pale.

"What we have to do."

"You mean bury him?"

"Can you think of something else to do with the body?"

Devon felt flustered. "But why hide this?"

"Because Covington will come looking for his friend, and I don't want him to find the body. Officially none of this ever happened. We never saw Mr. Sheedy. We were just coming back from Arthur's Pass. Didn't see anyone."

Devon looked at the others. They were as confused and scared as he. Two weeks ago everything had been perfect. They had made their little utopia. But day by day it had slipped away, and now they were in a nightmare.

"I guess we don't have a choice," Marcy said uneasily, looking to Reed for reassurance. "We'll have to rehearse a story."

"You're agreeing to all this?" Devon said to her. He was shocked.

"We have to," said Otis.

"Why? Why not tell the truth? Even if Covington has it in for us, it's better to be honest. It just feels right. It's what the club stands for. Once we start making up stories it'll never end. And it's too easy to be caught in a lie."

"I don't trust Covington for beans," Otis said. "Look what he did to our clubhouse. And he's always hated Reed."

"If we have a good, consistent story, we'll be okay," Marcy offered. "We're good at sticking up for each other." Benjy nodded his agreement.

Devon turned his back in exasperation. What about Reed's speeches about always telling the truth? Why should this be the exception? Devon could see he was in the minority. This was a crisis. Maybe there was no point in fighting everybody. Reed was the leader. As strong as were Devon's misgivings, he figured he had to give in.

Devon and the others watched as Reed did the digging. Then the four boys dragged the body into the grave. The shotgun was tossed on top. For a second everyone stood back, as if what had happened was finally sinking in. Benjy started to cry. Marcy looked dazed. Devon realized he'd never seen a dead person. It didn't quite seem real. Alive one second, gone the next. He stared at the body, waiting for Mr. Sheedy to come to life and proclaim this an elaborate hoax, a joke on Reed and the rest of them. But the body stayed limp and motionless. And not just anybody had been killed. Mr. Sheedy was the father of the twins. What were they going to tell Amber and Jade? Lie to them, too?

When Reed had finished shoveling the dirt on top he took Devon aside. "You know I can't go with you to town," he said.

"What are you talking about?" Devon asked.

"I'm heading back up the mountain. It's safer for me there. You're the leader now."

"Oh, no—"

"Devon, you can do it. You have to do it."

"Wait a minute. We're all supposed to stick together. We're a club, remember?"

"It's better for you guys if I stay up here. When Covington gets concerned about Mr. Sheedy, he'll blame me. Because I didn't come back that'll make me more of a suspect—and take the pressure off the rest of you. Just tell Covington that I went after the twins and never came back. Amber and Jade will confirm I was hurt. It's logical that I couldn't make it back to you guys. And you had to get to town for help. It all makes sense."

Devon dropped to a boulder and ran his hands through his hair.

"This will work," Reed promised. "No one's going to find the body. People have disappeared before in the Adirondacks, even experienced campers like Mr. Sheedy."

"And how are you going to survive?"

"My ankle will get better. And I know my way around. When things cool down I'll come back and defend myself."

Devon's foot pawed at the dirt. Things were moving too fast.

"I won't let you down," Reed said. "I've never let you down. Can you keep your end of the deal?"

Devon tried to clear his head. Reed was a friend, his best friend. He might be proud and stubborn, but he'd made sacrifices for the others. Organizing the clubhouse, fighting the town, trying to save the twins; now he was trying to save them. Then why was there doubt in Devon's mind? He was ashamed to tell Reed, or ask the others how they felt. Devon kept wondering if Reed hadn't wrestled the shotgun and used it to kill Mr. Sheedy. The last few days had been strenuous, there'd been pressure on everyone, Reed especially. Now there was a dead body. Reed's story of being helped by the mountain man—a man Reed had never trusted and who had never trusted Reed—was it true? Devon tried to be more positive. Reed's story *was* possible. Fletcher was a weird guy, inconsistent in his behavior, maybe capable of helping even someone he didn't like, especially if he thought Reed were in trouble, like Devon had been. And wasn't Devon the one who had claimed the mountain man could be trusted?

"You are telling me the truth—" Devon suddenly turned to Reed.

His friend squinted in disbelief. "Have I ever deceived you?"

"No, never," Devon replied. He pushed aside his doubts. He had too many other things to think about. They'd be at the cabin in a few hours. And Olancha the next afternoon. Confronting his parents no longer seemed like a big deal. The problem would be in facing Covington, alone, without Reed's help, and telling the lies Devon didn't want to tell. Was he really a leader? He looked at Reed, the strong, unflinching face, someone to admire. Devon thought of the debts he owed and the friendship with Reed he was still trying to prove.

"Okay," he said reluctantly, gazing in the direction of Olancha. "I'll do my best."

Reed slipped his arm around Marcy and led her away from the others. He felt closer to her now than ever—he needed her more than ever—yet he knew he couldn't go into town.

"I'll be back as soon as I can," he promised.

"Are you sure you should stay away? Your ankle—" she said, concerned.

"I'll sneak down a week from today. Let's meet at your house. Midnight, say."

"You're sure?"

"I won't forget. A week from today."

"I can let you know what's happening with Covington."

"That's great." Reed gently cupped his hands around her face. "Hey, relax. Everything will be fine. Just stick to the official story."

"Okay."

"Remember, it's us against them."

Marcy felt better. Part of her wanted to stay with Reed in the mountains, but it would mess up their plan. She didn't feel the same about herself and her family as when she'd left Olancha. Growing closer to Reed had made her feel more independent from her parents. She knew she'd jeopardize her relationship with them by telling lies, but she felt strongly about Reed. The shooting hadn't been his fault—Reed had almost been killed himself—and now they had to deal with it in a way to protect themselves. She could handle this. The pressure would be more than she was used to, but Reed had given her confidence. Marcy was determined not to disappoint Reed or herself. She'd realized she wanted more for herself. Reed had helped her to see that whether he knew it or not.

"I'll miss you, I love you," she said, kissing him. Sliding her arms into her backpack, she rejoined the others.

16

"Breakfast."

Motes of dust floated in the channels of window light. Devon wrestled with his bed covers, stirred awake, and finally glanced at his mother as she walked out of his room. He wasn't hungry. His eyes jumped to the crammed bookcases and his typewriter on the desk—he didn't want to go near it. He was so used to writing the truth whenever he rolled in a sheet of paper that now, thinking of what really had happened in the mountains, he recoiled. He didn't even want to be home. Taking that first shower had been great, so was eating a hot meal, but after a while all he could think of was how confined and uncomfortable everything was. Only it wasn't his home that had changed, he realized, it was him. Living with that stupid lie, he couldn't think of anything else.

When the four had returned from the mountains, at first their parents had been more relieved than angry. Devon had given the story to the sheriff about Reed vanishing after going to look for the twins. Mr. Higdon felt his son would survive because he was an experienced backpacker, and with the ranger dragnet, there was a strong chance he'd be found soon. Devon had expected the third degree from Covington, but the sheriff hadn't said much, had just taken random notes. He hadn't even mentioned Mr. Sheedy, except to say he had been up in the Adirondacks looking for his daughters.

Dressed, Devon gave his parents a distant smile and excused himself from breakfast. He knew they didn't like his moodiness. He'd tried to explain he was just concerned about Reed and kept the rest to himself. He not only felt guilty for lying to them, he could still vividly see Mr. Sheedy dead in that clearing. Devon felt bad now that he'd let Reed bury him up there. It was wrong, even if they were trying to protect themselves. The man deserved better—anybody deserved more than an anonymous grave. An uneasy Devon had avoided Otis and Benjy, and they had avoided him. Maybe they all wanted to forget the secret they were trying to keep. When would it ever be over?

He pedaled his bike listlessly toward the mountains. Anything to get out of Olancha. Passing workers at the lumberyard, he avoided their glances. The whole town knew Reed and Mr. Sheedy were missing. Devon was afraid of sudden questions, of people somehow looking through him and finding the truth. Reed had asked him to be the leader; Devon had responded by doing his best to avoid the world.

"Hey, Devon—"

His foot dragged the bike to a stop. He took a breath as Amber approached. They'd spoken on the day the rest of the club had returned. Amber had apologized for leaving the group early with Jade. They were tired and frustrated, she'd said. Now she saw it as no big deal.

"Where are you going?" she asked in a lonely voice.

"Just riding."

"Have you seen Marcy?"

Devon shook his head.

"She told me on the phone she was grounded. Even if she wasn't, I got the feeling she didn't want to see me. Just because we had a falling out doesn't mean we aren't still friends. How about Otis? Have you seen him?"

"No." Devon was eager to ride on.

"Why isn't everybody getting together? Aren't we still a club?"

"We're waiting for Reed to get back."

"I hope that's soon. I know he'll be furious with Jade and me, but we'll work it out. I hope my father gets back soon, too."

Devon nodded and jumped back on his bike. A dump truck with debris spilling over its top nearly pushed him off the road. As the old clubhouse came into view, he saw three men hefting sledgehammers, taking turns collapsing a wall. He'd almost forgotten it was being demolished. The severed wiring and plumbing dangled in the ruins. No windows, no roof. The few pieces of furniture left behind had become a pile of kindling. Devon felt helpless. It was as if more than a building were being destroyed.

From nowhere a hand dropped on his shoulder.

"Morning," Sheriff Covington said in a warm voice. The hand rotated back to his hip, brushing the holstered revolver. The uniform was darkened under the armpits but otherwise it was starched and spotless as usual. In contrast to the rundown town, the sheriff was spit and polish, a standard-bearer for what he thought others ought to be. There was nothing wrong with that kind of pride, Devon supposed. It just made him wonder why Covington was content to be a sheriff in a piss-ant town like Olancha. The sheriff was intolerant, but he wasn't a typical narrow-minded, small-town hick. He'd had a couple of years of college somewhere. The man was no dummy. He could have done a lot of things.

"Morning," Devon finally answered, crossing his arms over his chest.

The sheriff angled his neck to the Adirondacks, fixing on one spot, as if he could actually see something. "Worried?" he asked. The sun glinted off his badge.

"What?"

"About your pal."

"No. Reed will be all right."

"Hope so. Sure would like to talk to him," Covington allowed as he pulled a notepad from his pocket.

"About what? I already told you everything," Devon said carefully.

The faded eyes swam over Devon, looking for an opening. "Tom Sheedy hasn't come back. I'm not sure what to make of that."

Devon shrugged.

"I just got through talking to Marcy again. You know what? She gave me a different version this time."

Devon fought off the butterflies. "There's no *version*. What we told you were the facts."

"Marcy's changed hers a little."

Like how, Devon wanted to ask, but he was too smart to take the bait. This was Covington's lie, a trap, a test. He should have expected it. The first questioning session had been much too easy. "There's nothing for me to change," Devon said.

"You sure you didn't see anyone after Reed disappeared? No other campers, fishermen, hikers—"

"No. And no Mr. Sheedy."

"You said that like you had expected to see him."

"I did hear a helicopter early the morning we started down. It could have been a search team for us. It could have been a lot of things, including Mr. Sheedy. I don't know. We never saw the chopper."

"It *was* Mr. Sheedy. Rangers dropped him off after picking up his girls."

"Okay," said Devon.

"And after you heard the chopper you didn't see anyone, or hear a shotgun, or find evidence of a struggle. . . ."

"No, sir."

"You're positive you didn't see Reed after he left to find the twins?"

"Like I said before—he just vanished."

"No one else saw him either? Not Benjy or Otis or Marcy?"

"Absolutely not. The rest of us were together. I already told you."

Covington took careful notes anyway. It seemed forever before he put his pad away. Then he pushed a toothpick in his mouth. Was he acknowledging that Devon was a tough opponent, or was this just another round?

"Funny thing about Reed," Covington volunteered as he peeked back at Devon from his car. "You know how much he likes to play games."

"What do you mean?"

"Always been a game player. Basketball's just one. He likes to play with people, too. Put them on the spot. Challenge them. Challenge himself, too. He manipulates people to get what he wants, or tries to. Weren't for me he'd be sheriff of this town," Covington allowed with a chuckle. "Under all that seriousness of his, the kid wheels and deals."

Devon nodded. It was true.

"What sort of game do you think he's playing now?" Covington asked. "I mean, who's he trying to manipulate?"

"I don't know what you're talking about."

"Sure you do."

"No. Sorry."

"He's manipulating you, Devon."

"And how's he doing that, Sheriff?" he asked, a little defensive.

"If I knew all the facts I could tell you better. But you do know the facts, so maybe you can tell me."

"Reed's lost. I hope somebody finds him. That's all I know."

The lowest game of all, thought Devon. Turning one friend against another. Still, Covington had struck a nerve. There were a lot of unanswered questions. Devon wondered again why Reed hadn't returned with the others. Couldn't he as easily have fended off Covington's queries here?

The last clubhouse wall suddenly crashed down behind him, but Devon didn't even turn around.

17

Marcy propped her foot against the ticket booth. The neglected movie theater was scarred with graffiti, its marquee faded and punched with holes—why hadn't Covington torn *it* down instead of their clubhouse? No one in town gave the movie theater a glance. She supposed that was why Devon had asked to meet there. He wouldn't say anything more on the phone, as if he thought someone might be listening. Marcy sensed something was up. In general things weren't going well. She was still tired and disappointed from last night when she'd stayed up past two. Reed had promised to show at midnight, but the only sounds Marcy heard from her patio were motorcyclists cruising the streets, and Covington chasing them away. Had Reed forgotten his promise? Wasn't she important enough to him?

Marcy's homecoming had been rougher than she'd expected. Her parents never showed anger by screaming at her, but they had made their disappointment very clear. She could still hear her mother's voice. How could she have been so irresponsible and thoughtless? She'd made a promise to be home after a few days—didn't she think about her parents' feelings? Reed was a bad influence. Marcy had apologized, but she'd been grounded for two weeks anyway. She hadn't helped her cause any by defending Reed. It had been her decision to stay in the mountains, too, she told her parents. She was more independent than anyone gave her credit for.

Still, Marcy wondered if she was holding up that well. Not having Reed or the club for support made her feel vulnerable. Covington, notepad always in hand, kept dropping by with more questions. Was everyone getting picked on as much as she? Did the sheriff think she was the weak link in the club? And the way Covington took her parents aside on each visit, as if to convince them to work on her, too, made her angry.

"Hi," she called as Devon approached. It felt natural to reach out, and quickly he gave her a hug.

"Thanks for sneaking out," he said. "How are you doing?"

"All right." She forced a smile, then dropped it. What was the point in pretending? "Not so great. Reed was supposed to show last night."

Devon looked concerned. "You're sure?"

"It's been exactly a week. I wouldn't forget that."

"Don't worry, he'll be there tonight. Something must have happened in the mountains. Or maybe he saw Covington or Brody by your house—"

"Maybe," she said, hoping.

"Listen, we'll all get through this mess. The important thing is not to panic. Now what did you tell Covington? He said you changed your story—"

Marcy sighed. "He always has so many questions. He tries to force me into contradicting myself. I guess that's what you warned us about."

"What did you tell him exactly?"

"I've always said the last time any of us saw Reed was the morning he went after the twins. Covington said that Amber and Jade told him they ran into Reed all right, but that he wasn't hurt. The reason he gave up chasing them was that their father turned up and Reed backed off. I couldn't believe they told him that. Maybe they were just scared. Anyway, I wasn't thinking—the words just popped out. . . . I said there was no way Reed ran into their father then. 'How do you know that?' Covington snapped at me. 'How do you know what happened out there—you weren't around. Or were you? Or did Reed come back to camp afterward? And what do you mean, *then*?' He kept looking at me—so did my folks—just waiting out the silence. I got flustered and admitted I had seen Reed afterward. . . ."

Devon rolled his eyes.

"Devon, I'm sorry! I swore to Covington that I was the only one. No one else saw him. The four of us had divided up to search individually, I said. I saw Reed, I called to him, but he didn't see or hear me, and I couldn't catch up with him."

111

"Did you say you told Benjy or Otis or me?"

"I had to. Otherwise it wouldn't sound credible. . . . Does any of this really make that much difference?"

Devon began to worry. He'd already told Covington that nobody had seen Reed after he'd left for the twins. Now Devon would have to contact Benjy and Otis and see how widespread the damage was. "Did you tell Covington anything else?"

"I told him about the mountain man."

"We weren't supposed to mention him. It only complicates things."

"All I said was he lived in a cabin near where we camped. Is that so bad?"

"No matter how much you're pressured, don't breathe another word to Covington. Say you've told him everything. Say you're tired and want to be left alone. Your folks should understand. What can Covington do to you, anyway?"

"Maybe arrest me," Marcy said, scared of the thought.

"There's no evidence of anything. Just take it easy." Devon could see she felt badly for letting him and the others down. He gave her another hug for support. "Are you going to be okay?" he asked.

"I think so."

Nearing her house, Marcy moved quickly to the back door. Something caught her eye. Unbelievable, she thought, staring back at Covington. It was as if he were stalking her, waiting for her to make her move. He was leaning casually on his open car door, hat cocked back. Now her parents would know she'd sneaked out. They'd add yet

112

another week to her grounding, as well as give her those looks of disappointment which made her feel even worse.

"I don't want to talk to you," Marcy said as Covington approached. He followed her into the house. Her mother stood waiting, arms crossed over her chest, looking hurt. A tall, willowy woman with high cheekbones, she had the same fine blond hair as her daughter.

"Marcy, where were you?"

"I had to get out. I took a walk."

"Where to?" the sheriff asked, dropping on the living room couch as if this were his home.

"Nowhere." Marcy stared at him. Could he possibly have seen her and Devon together? She wouldn't put spying past the sheriff. How could her mother just let Covington in the house anytime he wanted? Marcy had complained that she didn't like the sheriff. According to her parents, he was just doing his job. "Why do you act as if you have something to hide?" they'd asked.

"I've got a few more questions about Reed," Covington said to Marcy.

Exasperated, she looked at her mother for help. "I've told him everything I know."

"That's what you said the first time," Covington broke in. "And the next time you told me something different."

"Well, now it's over. You know everything I know."

"I wish that were true," he said. "Every day Reed and Tom Sheedy are gone I worry a little more. Seems too much for coincidence. I think the two got into a little tangle. And you and the others know all about it."

Marcy turned to her mother. "May I go to my room, please?"

"Honey, talk to the sheriff."

"He's harassing me."

"Marcy, don't be rude!"

"Why won't he leave me alone?"

"Just answer one question for *me,*" her mother said before Covington could interrupt. "Have you really told the sheriff everything?"

Marcy felt her mother's worried but caring stare. "Mom, may I go?"

"Answer me, please."

Marcy stood straight and looked them each in the eye. "All right. I've told everything I know. Everything is the truth. I swear it. I'm not holding anything back—*okay*?"

Her mother surrendered and let her go. But the image of her mother's troubled face stayed with Marcy. She couldn't help feeling guilty as she closed the door to her room. The posters of rock singers and movie stars stared back at her. She had never lied to her mom, not like this. What was she doing? Marcy couldn't face anyone for the rest of the afternoon, and dinner wasn't much better. Her secret was hurting the whole family. Tell them, get rid of the pressure, she thought. But she wouldn't. She would be loyal to Reed.

Around midnight, when she was sure her parents were asleep, Marcy put on a sweater and stood outside. The lilac bushes stirred softly. Her parents' bedroom was dark. She thought of the special times she'd shared with Reed in the mountains, before the trouble began. She was sure Reed felt the way she felt. A silvery moon silhouetted the footpath from the gate to her back door. In the distance the Adirondacks rose in the night shadows, as if holding Reed back from her. She was resentful, baffled. She dropped on a step, chin in her hands, eyes drooping.

A flashlight brought her head up with a start.

Reed, she thought joyfully, rushing up. But when her eyes adjusted she saw her father's round, seamless face.

"What are you doing, sweetie?"

"Couldn't sleep, Dad," she said quickly, doing her best to sound cheery.

"Something you want to talk about?"

"No. Just one of those nights."

"You're sure?"

She hesitated. "Yeah. See ya." And giving him a kiss she went back into the house.

18

"**S**omeone to see you, Devon."

He turned at his desk, losing the place in his book. "The sheriff?"

"How did you know?" his mother asked.

"Lucky guess." Devon was prepared for Covington. After seeing Marcy yesterday he'd paid a visit to Benjy and Otis. The sheriff hadn't really hounded them, not like he had Marcy, and they hadn't deviated from the official story. "Hey, we're loyal," Otis had said, a little upset, as if he thought Devon had doubts about them. "Marcy is, too," Otis added. "I never said she wasn't," Devon answered. He'd gone home feeling guarded but hopeful.

The damage wasn't so widespread. Maybe he was capable of containing Marcy's stray admissions.

"You wanted to see me?" Devon shuffled into the small living room with its simple furniture.

Covington was standing by the open front door. His eyes lifted to Devon. "Like to talk to you in my office," he said, friendly enough.

Devon smiled reflexively. He didn't relish sitting in the lion's den, not all alone with the lion. "What's wrong with right here?"

"Paperwork's down at the jail."

"Paperwork?"

"I want to get your story in writing."

"You already took plenty of notes."

"I want to make it official. I want a sworn statement."

"Sure—why not," Devon said after a beat. He couldn't look like he had something to hide. "Back in a while, Mom."

At the jail his nerves didn't hold quite as steady. Never having been in trouble, he was a stranger there. Just walking in made him think he'd done something wrong. Despite a lone ceiling fan that labored noisily, the cavernous, sparse room was hot and stuffy. Holding cells with steel bars were on one side, empty now. Wallpaper, faded and peeling, covered most of the room. Plaster was broken in some spots, and there were water stains on the ceiling from roof leaks. Devon slouched in the chair across from Covington's immaculately maintained desk. He couldn't help noticing the incongruity. Like the town, the jail was in a state of permanent decay, yet the sheriff's desk was an oasis of order and cleanliness.

Covington handed him a ballpoint from his shirt pocket. "Go ahead," he ordered Devon, "write it down. Everything. Then at the bottom you sign it, swearing your statement is complete and true."

The tone of civility used in public was suddenly missing. The door opened. Devon gave an appraising glance to the sheriff's deputy as he pulled up a chair next to Devon. Brody lacked his boss's intelligence and wit. The heavyset, smiling deputy could follow rules but didn't know how to think for himself.

As he wrote, Devon realized his hand was shaking, that he was even short of breath. His hand glided faster across the page. Both men stared at him in the silence. Ridiculous, he thought. He had to be stronger than this. They were just trying to wear him down.

"Here you go," he said, finally pushing the legal pad back across the desk.

"Everything in here?" Covington said after he'd read Devon's story.

"I think so."

"Think so?" he snorted.

"To the best of my memory."

Covington read the statement again, then showed it to Brody. "You didn't mention the forty-five. Reed's dad said it's missing from his gun cabinet."

Devon stretched as he nodded. "Yeah, you're right. Reed did have it, come to think of it. What's so important about that? I didn't put down what clothes everyone was wearing, either."

"What did he bring the handgun for?"

"Hunt small game. He's got a license."

The sheriff made a notation on a separate page. "When he went after the twins, did he have the forty-five?"

Devon thought back. Reed had pulled the gun on Fletcher at the camp, he remembered that clearly. The next day, starting for home and running into Mr. Sheedy . . . yeah, Reed did have the gun. He'd seen it bulging under his shirt. "I don't remember, Sheriff."

Covington's face was growing impatient, as if he knew Devon was lying. He looked determined to get a full confession. Well, let him keep pushing, Devon thought. I'll push back.

"You think Marcy remembers?" Covington spoke out.

"What's that?"

"Told me she saw Reed *after* he left to look for the twins. And she told you and the others, too. . . ."

"Now that you mention it, I guess she did. Small detail."

"Small detail?" Covington narrowed his eyes. "And what about the forty-five? Another small detail? If Reed had his gun and ran into Mr. Sheedy . . ."

Devon squirmed in his chair. He saw himself back in the mountains, hearing the terrible blasts, running over to find Mr. Sheedy dead. Muffled by the rocks, could the .45 have made those noises, or just one of them?

"You think your friend's a killer?" Covington asked suddenly.

Devon forced a laugh. "And Grandma Moses robbed banks."

"Just suppose Reed is. I told you that no one really understands that kid. And I understand him better than you, Devon."

119

"Just what is it you understand?"

"When those two ran into each other, Reed got scared and shot Tom. Now he's so scared out of his mind he's hiding."

"He's lost."

"Hiding," Covington repeated.

"Sounds farfetched to me."

"What I don't know for sure, Devon, is how much you know."

"Absolutely nothing, Sheriff." He thought his heart would explode.

"You're his friend, Devon. You and your club pals think I'm an ogre, but I'll help Reed if you tell me where he is. You have to trust me."

Trust you, sure. Devon looked at Brody, too. He'd rather be at the mercy of stampeding elephants. The sheriff tapped a pencil against the legal pad, waiting.

"I wish I could help, Sheriff, but I wouldn't know where to look for Reed."

"There's something else Marcy told me. About a mountain man . . ."

"Sure. I put that in my statement."

"You left it out earlier."

"Another oversight. Sorry."

"Where's this mountain man live?"

"Got me. You'll have to ask Reed. I'm not very familiar with the Adirondacks."

"No idea at all? Just for the record I'd like to know where the man lives."

Sure you would, Devon thought. So you'd know where to start looking for Reed.

"You made friends with him?" the sheriff asked.

Devon said nothing. In some ways it was a pointless question, but then again it wasn't. Devon knew the sheriff's tactic now. He would take everything Devon said and go back to Marcy and ask *her* what happened. The ritual would go on indefinitely, back and forth, until the list of inconsistencies grew so remarkable that the sheriff would be able to begin to pin things down. And if their story didn't finally fall apart or crack wide open, one of them would.

"What was his name?" Covington asked in the silence.

"How would I know?"

"You know a lot more than you're telling me," he said more firmly. "You're stonewalling."

"No, sir."

"You're trying to be like Reed—taking on the whole world. Really you're a bundle of nerves, right under that cool surface of yours. You're just as weak as Marcy."

Devon felt a surge of anger. He masked it with a smile. The deputy suddenly got up and circled around Devon's chair. "You know what perjury is?" Brody asked.

"Yes, sir."

"Lying in a sworn statement . . ."

"I know."

Brody's fat, pompous smile wasn't laughable. Devon's mouth was so dry he could barely talk. "I've got nothing more to say, Sheriff. I've told you everything I can think of. I'd like to go now."

"Where to?" asked Covington.

"Home."

"Just don't go running off to the mountains."

121

"Why would I want to do that?"

"To tell Reed what's going on."

Or just to get away from you, thought Devon. He rose calmly and drifted outside. On a side street, out of everyone's view, he stopped and placed his trembling hands on his knees. Then he threw up. The thought of ever having to go through that with Covington or Brody again terrified him. All the lying he'd done made him feel like he was suffocating. He had to talk to somebody. His parents would never understand. Hugo? Maybe, but could he trust the newspaper editor? He was starting to sound like Reed.

Devon hurried home, filled a backpack, and without a note to anyone, headed into the mountains.

19

"You've got circles under your eyes." Marcy's father peered at her over his glasses as the family sat for dinner. "Didn't you finally get to bed last night?"

"Sure," she said noncommittally. She was still embarrassed her father had found her in the garden. She hadn't told him who she was waiting for. Marcy had already brought up her new feelings for Reed, only her parents hadn't paid much attention because their major concern was for Reed's survival. To discuss him any further wouldn't prove anything, Marcy knew, and she didn't really care if she had her parents' approval for a new boyfriend.

What she needed was to resolve her own feelings. Everything was in a holding pattern until Reed got back—or was it? Would Reed's appearance stop the conflicting thoughts and emotions she'd felt since coming home? Without the sheriff hounding her, she was finding time to put things in perspective. Maybe the reason she was embarrassed last night wasn't for what her father would think of her waiting for Reed, but for what she was thinking of herself. She wasn't independent at all. More and more she saw herself as a coward. Covering up Mr. Sheedy's death was wrong. The lie had always bothered her—her strong feelings for Reed had just allowed her to push away her doubts and rely on him. But really she had to rely on herself, and listen to her doubts. Allowing Covington to pick apart her story might not have been disloyalty to Reed or the club so much as a sign of being uncomfortable with the lie.

"Aren't you going to eat?" her mother asked.

"I think our Marcy needs a break. You want to come with me to Albany tomorrow?" her father said.

"What's in Albany?"

"I'm seeing Ed Watkins, the printer, about the winter catalog. I won't make it too boring for you. We'll go shopping and catch a movie afterward."

"Maybe," Marcy said. "What's so urgent with the printer?" Her parents ran a small mail-order catalog of camping and wilderness equipment, but the winter catalog wasn't usually printed until late summer.

"I like Watkins, but every time I want to make a last-minute price change, or introduce a new item, or allow back orders and exchanges, he thinks I'm making more work and expense for myself and for him. 'Come on, Frank,' he'll say, 'forget the public. You bust a gut for everybody, but they don't really care about you. Look at it this way, it's us against them.' "

"What?" Marcy said, suddenly paying attention. The words sounded familiar. Then she remembered her final parting with Reed.

"Watkins is a man with a siege mentality," her father continued. "He divides the world when it doesn't need to be divided. Making a war for himself that doesn't have to be fought."

"May I be excused?" Marcy said.

"What for? Where are you going?"

"Please, may I take a walk? I won't be long. I really need some air."

She grabbed a sweater and hurried toward Devon's. She entered through the back door and found him in his room. His parents were out. She stared at his dirt-streaked face and hands.

"Where have you been?" Marcy asked.

"In the mountains looking for Reed. I didn't find him," he said, dejected. "I hope he's not hurt worse than when we left him."

"My sense is Reed is fine. How are you?"

Devon dropped on his bed. "Bushed. And scared, if you want to know. Covington and Brody gave me the third degree this morning. But I didn't tell them anything," he said proudly.

"Why not?" she asked suddenly.

"What do you mean 'why not'? Because Reed's my friend. Because I'm loyal to him . . . like he's been loyal to me."

"How loyal is it if he abandons us?"

Devon sat up, surprised and annoyed. "Look, he didn't abandon us. We're all just following the plan. He'll be here soon."

"Oh, come off it, Devon," she said, just as sharply. "You've had the same doubts, admit it. That's the real reason you were out searching for Reed. I'm worried about him, too. Sometimes I think I might be in love with him. But I can't fight another feeling I have, too—there's a distinction between loyalty and doing what's right."

"Listen, I watched you two on the trip. I know you're hung up on Reed," Devon said. "That's your problem. You're mad at him now because you think you've been stood up. It hurts, sure. But it also makes you blind to the real issue."

"No, it doesn't. I'm seeing things clearly for a change. Mr. Sheedy was shot and killed. We had no right to bury him up there. You know the law as well as I do. You're supposed to be the investigative reporter—how can you turn your back on the truth?"

"Report this?" he answered, disbelieving. "You've got to be kidding. And get Reed in trouble?"

"He didn't kill Mr. Sheedy, so he'll be okay. We're here to stick up for him. I've been thinking about everything—especially Reed. He thinks everyone but the club is the enemy. That's just not true. When I'm with Reed I fall under his spell. He's wonderful, but he's not realistic. The world is bigger than Sheriff Covington."

"Why are you pushing this?" Devon demanded, flustered. "I know right from wrong, but we owe Reed. We owe it to talk to him before we agree to do anything."

"How long are we going to wait? Another few days? A

week? What if he never comes back? We have to live with ourselves. We have to face our parents.''

"Marcy, I don't believe you! You just said you loved Reed. Don't you even know what love is? And where's your faith? Are you a hypocrite?''

"All I know is I'm not waiting any longer. I can't. Maybe I don't love Reed that deeply. I'm really confused, but I do know I hate lying. I wanted to let you know that, before I tell my parents—''

Devon's jaw tightened. "Tell your parents? There's no way! They'll tell Covington. Think of Reed. Think of the club.''

"Devon, this isn't easy for me. I don't like Covington or giving in to him any more than you do. But not saying anything about what happened is a lot harder. What this comes down to is, I can't give Reed what he wants *and* live with myself. Reed will have to understand that. You're his best friend, so I want you to understand, too. Reed's asking too much of all of us. He wants us to put him before ourselves. You know how he always lectures us about being more independent? Well, I finally am.''

Devon took a breath to calm himself. "Marcy, hold off. Please. Give me another day to find Reed. Just one more day. I can do it, I know I can.''

Devon's pleading tone made Marcy feel all the worse, but she knew what she'd decided and there was no going back for her. She wiped a tear from her cheek and whispered good-bye.

═══20

Somebody was beating a drum. The louder the banging the deeper Devon tried to hide in the tissue-thin cocoon of sleep. Finally he bolted up in bed. As his eyes adjusted he could see that the sky was still dark.

More pounding. His glance flicked to the door as his parents entered in their pajamas and robes. Covington was a step behind them. He leaned against the doorjamb and spun his hat around his finger. "Sorry to have to disturb you, son . . ."

Devon's stomach began to turn as he came fully awake. He couldn't believe Marcy had actually done this. He hadn't prepared himself.

"Got a call from Marcy's mother late last night," Covington informed him. "Marcy finally admitted the four of you were with Reed when you ran into Tom Sheedy. Tom was shot dead, and you buried him right there—to cover things up."

"Now wait a second—"

The sweat beaded down Devon's neck.

"Until an actual body turns up," Covington went on, "we're keeping this under wraps, out of respect for Tom's family. You know Tom's family, Devon. His girls were in your little club."

Devon searched for something to say. He felt lost, defeated. "Then what do you need me for?"

"One, you perjured yourself. Two, we've got some gaps to fill in. Three, I've still got to find Reed. I promised your folks that if you cooperate I'll forget your perjury."

Devon felt like he was sleepwalking as he fumbled into his clothes and followed Covington outside. He gave his mother a kiss on the cheek and told her not to worry. He was amazed at how coolly he acted. Inside he was in a frenzy. He was stunned and hurt that Marcy had given the details to Covington. Yet hadn't he sensed from the start that their lie would never hold up? Benjy would probably be next. Without Reed the club had collapsed like a house of cards. Devon felt like a failure as a leader again, yet how could he have succeeded if he had to lead a pack of liars? The ordeal was hardly over. What was he going to tell Covington now? He knew one thing. Marcy had betrayed Reed but Devon wouldn't.

At the jail Covington fixed him coffee. Another legal pad was shoved toward him.

"This time give it to me straight." The sheriff's faded

eyes had taken on a glow. He was on a mission, something to elevate his job to new and important heights.

"What did Marcy tell you?" Devon wanted to know.

"I ask the questions, son. You do the writing. All you have to do is tell the truth."

Devon took the pen, played with it, and put it down. The ceiling fan whirled stubbornly. "I can't do it. Reed's my friend."

"I told you the last time—the smartest thing you could do is tell me where he is."

"Smart for who?"

"Don't you want Reed to have a chance to give his story?"

"He'll come down when he's ready." Devon pushed the yellow pad back to him.

"You don't understand, Devon. Unless you want to stay in trouble, you'd better tell me a few things."

Devon glanced to the empty cells. He stirred in his chair. Maybe it was crazy to hold out totally. Covington wasn't ever giving up. "Like what?" asked Devon.

"Marcy was a novice in the mountains. She wasn't sure where you built that lean-to. Arthur's Pass is a pretty big piece of real estate."

"I'm not sure, either," he said cautiously.

"How about where you buried Mr. Sheedy? Remember that?"

"No."

"Rangers are going up that way in an hour or so. Marcy knew approximately, but you'd know better. I want you to go with them."

"I wouldn't be of any help."

"Bull."

Devon looked away. He couldn't stand this. "Just supposing I do help. What's going to happen to Reed? You know that Reed didn't shoot Mr. Sheedy. Marcy must have told you that."

"Marcy told me what Reed told her. That some mountain man killed Tom. Justifiable homicide, Marcy claims, because Tom was about to shoot Reed . . ."

"That's right."

"Marcy said she didn't see the shooting. Did you?"

Devon was forced to shake his head.

"Nobody did, right?"

"Reed did."

"You're taking his word?"

"Yes," said Devon.

"Then why did you bury the body and lie to me?"

"You hate Reed. You'd never believe the truth."

"You're right about that. Because that *wasn't* the truth. Let me tell you what really happened. Reed shot Tom with his father's forty-five. All I have to do to prove that is find the body and dig out the bullet. You don't have any objections to that, do you? You've got an open mind. . . ."

No objections, thought Devon, as long as he could trust Covington. That was a big risk. All he knew for sure was that the sheriff hated Reed, and this was the perfect opportunity for putting Reed in his place—off Olancha's streets forever. "I've got an open mind, Sheriff. I was just wondering if you do, too. When you find the body, who's going to examine it with you?"

"I'm the sheriff here."

"The shooting was on state land."

131

"I'll call in state forensics for verification."

Maybe, thought Devon, maybe not.

Covington slouched back in his chair. Almost amused by Devon's defiance. He knew he had all the time in the world. He'd gotten Marcy to confess and now he'd pick off the others, one at a time.

"Tell me about Tom's shotgun," Covington spoke up. "How many shots were fired?"

"Two. No, one . . ."

"Which is it?"

"One from Mr. Sheedy, another from Fletcher."

"Says Reed, right? Did you check the barrel chambers afterward?"

"No."

"Why not?"

"Why should I have?"

"If they're both spent and we find fresh powder tracings, that means Reed lied. Maybe Reed didn't use his forty-five. Maybe he wrestled away Tom's gun and shot him with that."

"He didn't. He doesn't lie."

"Until his hand is forced."

"You don't know him at all," Devon huffed.

"I know this much. He's getting you in lots of trouble."

"If I'm in trouble, it's my problem."

"You know better than that. It's Reed who caused all this. Got himself in trouble, too. You really think some mountain man came to his rescue? That's just a dream, a fairy tale. Reed lives in a fantasy world. He's got what he calls 'high ideals,' but they aren't rules society can live by. They're too high even for him. They get him into impossible situations that only his fantasies can get him out of. . . ."

Devon sat with the coffee mug in his hands. He hated the silence and Covington's searching eyes. He hated the possibility that Covington, his enemy, might be right.

"Maybe it wouldn't even matter if you told me where Reed was," Covington suggested. "My bet is he's long gone."

"Yeah, sure."

"He's running. Bad ankle or not, he's running. He's strong and smart enough to know he couldn't stick around the mountains. He'd be found sooner or later. What's it been now, more than a week? We've had search teams up. Couldn't find anything. Kid probably sneaked into Wayne Junction and hitched to New York City."

Devon was furious at the suggestion. "Reed will be down any day."

"To save you?"

"That's right."

"Listen to me, Devon. Reed threw you to the wolves. The minute he convinced everybody to head home while he stayed in the mountains—that's when you should have known. Reed must have really had you buffaloed. But it's always been that way, hasn't it?"

Devon told himself not to listen. Still, he remembered Reed's argument about taking the pressure off them. It hadn't turned out that way.

"You don't scare me," Devon said defiantly.

Covington rose and pulled the cell keys from a desk drawer. "Oh, you're scared all right. And jail time will scare you more. Wait till you go before a jury for obstruction of justice—''

You can't lock me up, Devon started to say, but he knew Covington could do as he pleased. This was his town.

"I want to see Otis and Benjy," Devon protested as he was pushed into the cell. "Or call my parents."

"I'd better explain something," Covington allowed as the key turned in the lock. "You don't have a helluva lot of rights here. You aren't in your club anymore. The club's gone. This is the real world. A man was killed. The father of two of your friends. When are you going to face reality?''

Reality? thought Devon, dropping on the hard mattress. If Covington meant Olancha, reality was a joke. Covington left the building. Alone, Devon started to feel like he was suffocating again. He thought of the mountains, how much he wished he were up there. Anything to escape. Absurdly, he tried to squeeze his lanky frame through the narrow bars, straining till the blood left his face. Then he surrendered and dropped on the mattress, closed his eyes, and waited for Reed.

21

Around three o'clock Covington returned to the jail. Sheepishly Devon's parents marched in behind him.

"Where have you been?" Devon demanded when Covington left them alone. "How could you let him do this to me? You have to get me out—"

His mother looked pained, almost embarrassed. "The sheriff asked us to talk to you."

"I've nothing to say. Just get me out. Call a lawyer."

"Why won't you cooperate?" his father asked. "You've been lying to everybody. You've never done that in your life. I don't know what your motives are, but we're talking about a murder. . . ."

"That's why I need a lawyer! Look, Covington's denying me my rights. I haven't eaten all day. It's ninety degrees in here . . ."

"Just calm down, okay?" said his father. "You know there're no attorneys in town."

"Then call someone in Wayne Junction."

"I'll see what I can do."

His mother still looked distressed. "If you'd just go with the rangers and find the body, you'd be out of trouble," she argued. "It's Reed the sheriff wants to talk to."

"Wants to frame," Devon corrected. "And maybe me, too."

"Why would he care about you?"

"Don't you see what's happening?"

"You didn't shoot Mr. Sheedy, did you?"

"Of course not!" How could his mother even think that? "Listen, Covington has never liked our club. If Reed doesn't come back right away he's going to pick on someone else. Me. I'll be the scapegoat—"

Devon stared at the blank, uncomprehending faces. He couldn't believe they weren't taking his side. Did they think he was still covering up? Communication at home hadn't been great the last year, that's why the club had been so important, and Reed's friendship so reliable and comforting. But in a crisis, couldn't he expect his own parents to stick up for him? Maybe not. No wonder he needed to count on his friends.

"Why won't you get me out of here?" he asked.

"I'll see what I can do," his father repeated.

"What did Covington tell you?"

"That Reed killed Mr. Sheedy."

"It's a lie. A hermit named Fletcher shot him. To save Reed's life."

His father's jaw twisted back and forth in deliberation.

"Dad, who do you believe? Covington or me? I was there. And I know Reed . . ."

Covington suddenly reappeared. Devon's parents were reluctant to talk anymore. When the door closed behind them, Devon was alone with the sheriff again.

"Your folks change your mind?"

"No," he said stubbornly.

"Too bad." Covington leaned against the cell bars, his face screwed up to meet Devon's. He could see the sheriff's patience wearing thin. "I spent two hours with Otis and Benjy today. They say they don't remember where the body was buried. I believe them. Otis was too sick to remember, Benjy too young. Rangers just came back. Empty-handed again. That means I still need your help."

"I wouldn't hold my breath if I were you."

For the first time Covington looked frustrated enough to do something physical to Devon. "You're going to starve to death in my jail, boy."

"I'm still not going to help."

"The charges are going to be more than perjury and obstructing justice. You're an accessory to murder. I'll get Marcy or Benjy to say you and Reed conspired to murder Tom. Reed had a gun, he had opportunity, and he sure had a motive, because everyone knew he and Tom didn't get along. You were his accomplice."

"Go to hell, Sheriff."

Covington smiled tightly. "Got you thinking, don't I? Well, think about this, son. You know the real reason you don't want to find that body? Because we're going to discover a forty-five slug or Tom's own birdshot in him. That would mean Reed had duped you all along. You'd know then he was never coming back, that he's running hard, that you're not even on his mind—''

"Get out of here."

"—you'd know you've been sacrificed, and all because you were worrying about being loyal to Reed.''

"Shut up!''

"I'll be back, son.''

Devon knew he could count on that—Covington would always be back. In the silence and the heat Devon thought he was losing his mind. He refused to believe that Reed had deserted him and the others. The rest of the world might be screwed up, but not the club, not what it stood for. That had to be real, because if it wasn't, what else did he have to believe in?

The banging again. It was no drum this time. The sound was metallic, a deep, sonorous clanging, like someone ringing a bell. Devon flicked one eye open. He tried to sit up, but there were cramps in his legs from being curled on the short cot. A single light shining over Covington's desk revealed an empty chair. Devon's eyes focused closer in. The deputy's slovenly figure was in the shadows, his billy club clanging against the cell bars.

"What are you doing?'' Devon asked, rubbing his eyes. As he pulled himself up, his stomach spun with hunger.

"Too much sleep is bad for you.'' Brody flashed his toothy grin.

"Where's Covington?''

"Home, I guess."

"What are you doing here?"

Brody produced a key and entered the cell. "Boss said you're not cooperating."

A coppery taste flooded Devon's mouth. "I don't have to talk to you."

"Yes, you do. You talk to me."

"I want to see Covington."

"You're going out tomorrow and find that body for us, aren't you?"

Devon struggled to come fully awake. "Okay," he said after a moment, "I'll go with the rangers tomorrow." Fat chance, he thought.

The deputy answered by swinging his club down. The surprise blow glanced off Devon's ear and he shrank back on the mattress.

"I'm having a hard time believing you, Devon."

"I said I'd do it, didn't I?"

Brody was suddenly in a heat. "You think I'm stupid, don't you? All you kids do. You tell me one thing now, then you'll change your mind in the morning—"

"No," Devon swore, to appease him. "No change."

"Do tell," Brody said with a nod, and moved closer.

22

"**M**arcy, come out of the kitchen," her mother called from the living room. "You've been there all afternoon."

"I can't, the pie's almost ready for the oven. And what about dinner? Dad's coming up the steps . . ."

"I'll finish the supper. All you've been doing is working—"

"No, I'll do it."

Marcy didn't want to come out. She'd always enjoyed cooking and baking. She remembered the last time she'd spent any time in the kitchen. It was to make fried chicken for the club's second anniversary. The party seemed so long ago. Without the club and a place to hang out she'd begun to hate the free time of summer. There was nothing

140

to do. Last night, without any pleasure, she'd told Covington everything. Did her friends think she was a traitor? Tomorrow she would tell them that she had done what she felt was right. She would do the same thing again. Her parents, relieved, forgave Marcy and acted like this would be the end of the terrible business. Marcy knew better. When would the body be found? What about Reed? Her head was spinning from thinking so much about him.

Marcy laid the pie on a cookie sheet and listened to her parents' hushed voices in the next room. Devon was being held by Covington. The stubborn boy wasn't cooperating. The rangers had come back without finding a body. Marcy worried. What was Covington doing to Devon? Why was he being as stubborn as Reed? Why couldn't he see that the law was the law?

After dinner Marcy slipped out of the warm house and sat in the garden. The sky was a canopy of black and silver. She watched the flickering television through the curtains. After a while her father rose and switched it off.

"Marcy—"

Her head swung around.

"Over here."

She rose uncertainly. Then she saw him. She stepped back.

"What's the matter?" Reed said, almost playfully, as he approached. "Hey, I'm no ghost—"

Reed looked so different, she thought. Even in the darkness she could see that he was cleaned up, shaved, and he wasn't limping. The broad shoulders looked relaxed, the handsome face, concerned and studious. It was

141

as if he'd never been in the mountains, as if their ordeal had never happened.

He came up and hugged her.

"Please don't," she said after a moment, pulling away.

A look of confusion replaced his smile. "What's the matter? Hey, I'm sorry I'm late, but I couldn't get past the rangers till this evening. Just now, I managed to sneak into my house and clean up. You're the first person I've seen—"

"Sit down," she said, taking his hand.

"How come you look so mad? I followed the plan. I did the best I could. I'd never have let you down. You didn't think that, did you?"

"I'm not mad," she said. "I'm uncomfortable. This is hard for me."

Reed blew out of the corner of his mouth, waiting.

"I told Covington everything," Marcy said as she met his eyes.

Reed squinted in disbelief.

"I know you'll think I let you down, but I couldn't let myself down," she said. "I thought about this long and hard, Reed."

"I trusted you," he said in a shaken voice. "You said you loved me. I let myself love you. I have real feelings for you. You said in the mountains you'd always stick up for me—"

"I know. I meant it at the time. I cared for you. I still do. But when I started to think everything over, I realized I'm not sure what love is, but I do know what truth is. I'm sure of that. I've always been attracted to your good looks, your ideals, your leadership—but I have to see myself for what I am and what I want and what I think is right. You helped me learn that. Can't you understand?''

"No," he said. His eyes glared at her. "You betrayed me. You betrayed everyone."

"It's not true! I need friends. Everybody does. The club was and is important to me. But friends or a leader can't be used as an excuse not to choose between what you think is right and wrong."

"You mean all I am is an excuse?" Reed said. The hurt shone in his eyes. "I'm in love with you. Doesn't that mean anything?"

"It means a lot to me. It means I want to help you. I want you to go to Covington and tell him what happened. I'll go with you. We're all behind you. Poor Devon's in jail because he's protecting you. That's not right—"

"I can't do that," Reed interrupted.

"Because you're too proud and stubborn? Because you can't trust anyone? Reed, all your ideals, your need to lead the club, your thinking that you care for everybody and you're so responsible and blameless while everyone else lets you down—it's almost a game, isn't it? It's a way to make you feel superior. It's a way for you to cover up your loneliness and fears. You don't want anyone to know you're as vulnerable as the rest of us are."

Marcy could feel the pounding in her chest. She had finally said it all. Even as she was standing up to Reed she still cared about him—much more than he realized. She watched his face change, and it was obvious he felt she'd let him down. There was nothing she could say or do to change his mind.

"Please don't run away," she said as he turned brusquely.

143

Michael French

"You have too much going for you. You can still get a basketball scholarship. You can make it big. I know this is hard for you, but I faced up to my challenges. You can, too."

She started toward him only to have Reed step back, his hands held up in a warning to stay away. Then he turned and ran.

23

The billy club rushed down. Devon's knees crumpled, and he descended into a swirling blackness. He tasted his own blood. No more, he begged, but the words didn't come out.

He looked up with fear and hate. Brody cocked the billy club back again. Devon thought of trying to overpower him, but that was a dream. Maybe this whole thing was a dream—only when would he wake? How could his parents have deserted him? Were they trying to teach him a lesson?

His hands covered his head and the fear pushed up from his stomach as he waited. Would Brody strike a second blow? Instead a shadow darted over him. Something stirred on the far side of the room. Brody began to shuffle back in a crazy dance, his voice pitched in pain.

Devon blinked as he looked up. "Reed," he whispered. Reed held his hand out. The other had Brody's arm pinned back in a wrestling hold.

Devon admired how calm Reed looked. Just like when Reed had come for him when he'd fallen off the rockface onto the boulders.

"Time to get out of here," Reed ordered.

Devon struggled up. He was surprised he could even walk. He wanted to cream Brody. As Devon limped out of the cell, Reed shoved the deputy onto the mattress and locked him in. Brody's swearing crescendoed into shouts for help.

Outside, Devon gulped the fresh, cool air like it was water. His head throbbed and his mouth and nose were still bloodied, but somehow he felt great. When he had his breath back he focused on Reed. It wasn't a dream. "You really did come back."

"Was there any doubt? Sorry it took so long," Reed said, as they started running from the sheriff's office.

"Covington tempted me to give up on you, but I didn't," Devon said proudly. He remembered his doubts in jail. As he looked at Reed they vanished. "I knew you'd come through."

"And you came through for me," Reed replied, giving Devon's arm a squeeze of gratitude. "Wish I could say the same for Marcy."

"You saw her?"

"Forget about her. Some friend." His voice trailed off. "It's you and me now. Let's hurry before Brody wakes the town."

"What do you mean?"

"Time to escape, Devon."

"Where to?"

"The mountains for now."

Devon pulled to a stop. Puzzled, Reed fell back, and they stood, out of breath, at the base of the mountains. A mist wrapped around the tapered tops in an eerie beauty. "What are we going to do up there?" Devon asked.

"Lay low," Reed said with his usual confidence and logic. "As of tomorrow there'll be rangers and state police combing every meadow, valley, and forest on the mountain. When it's clear, we'll sneak away, maybe down to Albany. From there we can get to New York City. Come on, let's hustle," he said impatiently.

And after New York City, then where? Devon wondered. It felt like they were on their first trip again— running away, running for the sake of running, running from something just because they didn't like it. All running had gotten Devon was into trouble.

"I don't know," Devon said. "I need to think a minute."

"Think about what?" Reed asked, exasperated. "There's no time. What—are you pulling a Marcy on me?"

Devon resented that. He'd gone through a lot for Reed. He felt he'd paid back all the debts he owed his friend. And maybe Marcy wasn't such a villain. In his cell he'd had plenty of time to think about what she'd done, how hard it must have been for her. "I just want to think," Devon repeated, more insistently.

"Hey, I just saved your life. You were being beaten to a pulp. You want to go back to that?"

Devon wagged his head.

"Then what choice do we have?"

147

There were choices, Devon realized. Maybe he couldn't go back to Covington or even expect his parents to help, but what about Hugo? The newspaper editor had always been fair. Devon would tell him everything, and insist everyone get a fair hearing. Devon wished he'd gone to him before all the lying had started. Maybe the world would always be screwed up, but no matter what, Devon still believed that some people were capable of being honest. He'd held on to that hope even during the worst of times. He'd had to make so many choices, but at least he'd seen he had choices. Hard choices maybe, but choices nonetheless. Maybe Reed's problem was that he had never really made choices; he just got himself in tough situations and felt the only way out was running.

Devon was surprised at how calm he felt. "Reed, I can't go with you."

"Don't get crazy on me, Devon."

"I can't. Your way is a dead end. I'd like to live with a little hope."

"What are you talking about? What hope do you see in Olancha? Are you with me or not?" he demanded.

"I'm not going."

Reed's look of amazement turned to disgust. "After all we've done together. It's incredible. You're just like Marcy—"

"Tell me one thing, Reed," Devon spoke up. "I want to know if you really killed Mr. Sheedy."

"So that's it. Now you believe Covington instead of me."

"I don't believe Covington. I never will. It's you I want to believe."

"I already told you."

"The truth?"

Reed blew nervously out of the corner of his mouth.
"Hey, who do you think you're talking to?"

"A friend."

"That's right. Someone who's always helped you."
Reed smiled reflexively, but the smile didn't extend to his
eyes. "So why are you talking to me this way?"

"Did you shoot Mr. Sheedy?"

Reed fidgeted with his hands.

"Just tell me," Devon raised his voice. "Yes or no?"

His friend's lips moved soundlessly.

"Tell me, damn it!"

"You wouldn't understand," came a suddenly tired
voice.

Devon dropped on the cold ground.

"You can't understand, Devon! You aren't me! You
weren't there!" Reed's face grew animated. "This is the
story. I was scared. I was exhausted. I was hurt. I couldn't
stand the pressure. I'm not Superman, okay? I thought Mr.
Sheedy was going to kill me—I swear it! I wrestled the
shotgun away. One barrel went off as we fought, then I
pointed the gun at him— What would you have done?"

"I don't know. Maybe I would have killed him, too.
But you should have told me and the others. We would
still have stuck by you. You tried to make all of us believe
you were invincible. You made the mistake." He studied
Reed's isolated figure against the massive mountains.

"I told you that you wouldn't understand," Reed said.

"You know, I always thought I wanted to be like you,
Reed. You were my ideal, my model. I really envied you.

149

Michael French

It seemed to me you had so much more than the rest of us.
But down deep I couldn't quite identify with you, not
totally, even if I'd wanted to. I just couldn't pinpoint the
difference between you and me—''

''Devon, I really need you now. Okay? I'm not invincible. I admit it. Now you know. Please, don't leave me.''

''—the difference, Reed, is that I care and I always have.
You don't. You care about principles maybe, but not
people, not your friends, not until you desperately need
them like now.''

''Look, I made a mistake with Mr. Sheedy. I made a
mistake with you. I said I'm sorry! I was only protecting
myself. Is that such a crime? I care about friends. I do.''

''Then tell Hugo exactly what happened. If you care
about other people you have to trust them too. Have you
really considered how far it's possible to run?''

''You're telling me I have to take my chances alone?''
he said, defiant. ''Fine. I always have with my life. I
couldn't count on my father. I can't count on you. But I'm
not going to Hugo and his little newspaper. I'll make it
my own way.''

Devon looked at him sadly. ''I've heard you talk about
not wanting to be like your father. But you know what?
You're going to be just like him after all. You'll always be
running.''

''Devon, you're just trying to get me when I'm down.
That doesn't sound like you care about me.''

''I do care. But you aren't listening.''

''Prove you care.''

''Come with me and tell your story to Hugo.''

150

"We've just been through that . . ."

"I'll take care of everything. I promise. No one's going to hurt you."

Reed gave a half laugh. *"You're* going to protect *me*?"

"Just come with me. It's the best way."

"Too late, Devon."

"Don't say that. Things will work out if you face them. Marcy and I will testify how Mr. Sheedy bullied and baited you. Otis and Benjy, too. The club isn't dead. We do have ties to each other. You're just not the leader anymore. We can now be equals."

Devon waited for the confusion and doubt on Reed's face to change to some kind of trust. Instead he hardened and looked even more defiant. "Bye, Devon . . ."

Reed pivoted, dug his boot into the soft dirt, and disappeared into the darkness. Devon blinked back a tear. Then he went the other way.

ABOUT THE AUTHOR

MICHAEL FRENCH is a native of Los Angeles. He attended public schools in that city and was graduated with a degree in English from Stanford University in 1966. He later received a graduate degree in journalism from Northwestern University. He currently lives in Santa Fe, New Mexico, with his wife, Patricia, and their two children, Timothy and Alison. Time permitting, he is a serious mountain trekker who favors exotic and remote destinations, among them New Guinea, the Amazon, Java, and Rwanda. Michael French is the author of a number of adult books as well as four young adult novels, *Soldier Boy, Lifeguards Only Beyond This Point, Pursuit,* and *The Throwing Season.*